Prima Donna

Book 1 & 2

McKinley's Journey

By Keisha Ervin

Prima Donna ~McKinley's Journey

P. O. Box 2535
Florissant, Mo 63033

Copyright ©2015 by
Prioritybooks Publications

Edited by: Kendra Koger

Cover Designed by Sheldon Mitchell of Majaluk

Manufactured in the United States of America
Library of Congress Control Number: 2015931876

ISBN: 978-0-9896502-1-2

For information regarding discounts for bulk purchases, please contact Prioritybooks Publications at 1-314-306-2972 or rosbeav03@yahoo. com.

Prima Donna McKinley's Journey

Prioritybooks
Publications

Dedication

To My Dear Beautiful Son,

I have a confession to make. I wasn't sure about you at first. To me you were just this extraordinarily handsome baby that smelled nice, most of the time. When you were first born I never realized how much being a parent changes you. I don't remember the exact moment things changed; I just know that they did. One minute I was just drifting along through life, believing I was invincible. The next, my heart was beating outside of my chest, exposed to the elements of the world. Loving you has been the most profound, extreme, heart-wrenching and fulfilling experience of my life. As your mother I made a silent vow to protect you from the world. And in many ways I have failed, but I promise from this day forward that I will do better. It's me and you, Buddy, 'til the end and if don't nobody else love you, you know Mommy's gonna love you 'til the end of time.

Acknowledgments

Father God, thank You for bringing me through once again. Your love and mercy are my covering and I thank You. I pray that I continue to live my life according to Your Word and not my own. Help me not to respond, but to react. Order my steps, God, and bless me to come through this trying time in my life victorious.

To my G4L girls: Locia, Tu-Shonda, Monique and Sharissa, thank you ladies for being such great friends. You all are more like sisters to me. I have really seen over the last month how much you all really and truly care for me. I couldn't have asked God to bless me with a better crew. Love you, dolls!

Mama, Daddy, Keon and the rest of the Poe and Ervin families, I love you.

Brenda Hampton, you are the best agent a girl could ask for. Over the years you have not only become my partner in crime, but a mentor and friend. You are a great role model and I can't wait for your memoir to drop so the world can see just how blessed you are. I love you!

Mrs. Rose Beavers, thank you once again for the opportunity to write a story for you. Working with you is always a pleasure. I wish you and your family nothing but success.

And to my loyal fans, thank you all for riding with me once again. I promise if it wasn't for y'all and me needing a paycheck I wouldn't be doing this. Your kind words of encouragement keep me going. I love each and every one of you from the bottom of my heart.

Keisha Ervin Contact Info:

www.wix.com/kyrese99/keishaervin
www.facebook.com/keisha.ervin
www.twitter.com/keishaervin
keisha_ervin2002@yahoo.com

Part One

"*I know you're mad at me, but baby, I'm so sorry.*"

Teedra Moses

"*No More Tears*"

A slight smile graced the corners of McKinley's lips as she rode down Washington Avenue. She couldn't have asked for a better night. The sun was setting perfectly over the horizon. Hues of orange and pink were in the sky. For a Miami spring night the temperature outside was a perfect seventy-eight degrees. Normally, it was scorching outside, but thankfully she was able to rock the Herve Ledger iron-dust color, strapless, form-fitting bandage dress and Ruthie Davis double-platform shoeties with spikes and Swarovski crystals she'd bought especially for that night.

It was a special evening, so she had to look her best. It was April 5th, her fiancé Jamil's thirty-first birthday. McKinley had an entire evening of surprises in store for him. They would attend a Heat's game, but before that, they'd have dinner and drinks at the ultra-exclusive restaurant B.E.D.

B.E.D, which stood for beverage, entertainment and dining, was a Miami staple and located in the middle of South Beach's nightlife district. Famous as a fine dining epicenter, B.E.D boasted large mattresses and mountains of pillows with the luxury of seclusion at the pull of a drape—a perfect setting for a decadent French-style cuisine with a Brazilian influence.

McKinley sat in the backseat of the Lincoln Town Car that Eduardo, her chauffeur for the night, drove her around in. As she checked her face, the reflection staring back at her from her Chanel compact confirmed what she'd expected. She was an absolute vision of perfection. Realizing they were getting close to the restaurant, McKinley placed her compact back inside her Judith Leiber birdcage minaudiere.

Seconds later, they pulled up to the restaurant's doors. Eduardo parked the car and hopped out to open McKinley's door. With the door opened, Eduardo leaned forward and extended his right hand.

"Thank you." McKinley placed her hand in his and stepped out.

As always, wherever she went, McKinley caused traffic to stop. All eyes were on her. Pedestrians on the street just had to catch a glimpse of the golden goddess. McKinley's distinct facial features were captivating. Everything about her was mesmerizing. She possessed brown doe-shaped eyes, deep dimples and pink pouty lips that complimented her honey-colored skin and ravenous long black hair.

She was a five-foot-four, curvy size ten. Sometimes the perception of what people thought she should be, because of her looks, was mind-boggling. McKinley constantly felt the need to stay on her "A" game. There was no way she could be caught dead in an outfit from last season or without her hair and nails done, or a face beat to perfection. In Miami, looks were everything and beautiful women like McKinley came a dime a dozen.

One false move and her social status could go from the

A-list to the D-list in a matter of seconds. Most importantly, chicks were dying to take her place. They craved the lifestyle Jamil showered her with and would do anything to get him in the sack. That was why that evening was so important. McKinley was determined to show him just how much she loved and appreciated him. After giving her reservation info to the maître d', McKinley was escorted to her bed, which was in the center of the room.

"Ugh," she said nervously. "Maybe this wasn't such a good idea." McKinley held onto the hem of her dress and climbed onto the bed.

Her dress was so constricting that as she scooted she lost her balance and fell forward onto her face.

"Ooh." She pushed herself back up.

"Are you alright, ma'am?" the maître d' asked, stifling a laugh.

"Yeah." McKinley blew her hair out of her face, praying her makeup wasn't smeared.

"Your server will be with you shortly."

"Okay." McKinley sat on her butt and crossed her legs.

A young Puerto Rican man with curly black hair introduced himself. "Hello. My name is Juan. I will be your server for tonight. Would you like to start off with something to drink?"

"I'll just have water for right now. I'm waiting on my boyfriend to arrive. It's his birthday." McKinley smiled.

"How wonderful." The server smiled back. "I'll be right back with your drink."

"Okay," McKinley said, glancing around the restaurant.

The atmosphere at B.E.D was dope. Pink and blue lights were dimmed low to give the space a sultry Moroccan appeal. The music was pumping and drinks were being served by the dozens. Nothing but the hottest and wealthiest people surrounded her. Everyone seemed to be enjoying themselves and having a grand time. McKinley couldn't wait for Jamil to arrive.

Twenty minutes later, McKinley sat on her bed alone, checking her watch, wondering where Jamil was. She'd reminded him just an hour before that they were to meet at seven on the dot. Frustrated, McKinley pulled out her cell phone and called him. He answered on the third ring.

"What up?" he said with a laugh.

"Where are you?" McKinley said low into the phone as she heard voices and music in the background.

"Hi, to you, too," Jamil shot back sarcastically.

"Where are you?" McKinley said impatiently.

"Why?"

"Ummmmm, 'cause I'm sittin' at the restaurant, waiting on you. What you mean why?" McKinley shot back with an attitude.

"I'll be there in a minute."

"What's a minute, Jamil?" McKinley rolled her eyes as Jamil laughed.

"Hello?" she snapped, knowing damn well he wasn't laughing at her.

"Ay yo!" Jamil shouted to someone.

"Jamil!" McKinley raised her voice, causing people around her to stare.

"Yeah," he answered.

"Are you seriously ignoring me, and who are you talkin' to?" McKinley fumed.

"Chill out. I said I would be there in a minute," he replied sternly.

"Well, please hurry up."

"Okay, I'm leaving now."

"I'm for real, Jamil. Come on."

"I said a'ight," he huffed.

"Bye," McKinley said, ending the call.

Thirty minutes later, she sat staring absently out into the crowd. *This nigga ain't coming,* she thought. Jamil had played her once again. She'd called him at least five times, but he didn't even bother to pick up. She wished she could say this scenario was all new to her, but it wasn't. Jamil's personality reminded of her Dr. Jekyll and Mr. Hyde. One minute he was this sweet, attentive man, and then in the blink of an eye he'd turn into an absolute monster. With him, she never knew what she was gonna get.

He'd taken her through it all. In the three years they'd been together, she'd dealt with him messing around on her, his constant lies and never keeping his word. Disappointed that all of her planning and dolling herself up had been reduced to shit, McKinley placed an order to go then called Eduardo. A while after that, she was home, kicking off her heels. The feel of the cold marble floor soothed her aching feet. The sight of McKinley's apartment always made her feel warm inside.

The burnt orange, tufted sectional, wooden coffee table, Nani Marquina Seagrass rug and three-panel painting by Christina Narwicz set the whole living area off right. McKinley walked into the kitchen, which was connected to the living room. The tears that had been begging to fall slid down her pink blush colored cheeks. She'd put so much time and effort into planning the perfect birthday celebration for Jamil, but now he wasn't even answering her calls. As she stood crying, McKinley could not come to grips with the concept that Jamil could be that blatantly disrespectful.

At this point in their relationship, they should've been beyond all of the petty nonsense. He should have known that his actions would affect her in a negative way. He should have known that her heart felt like it was being choked with his bare hands. He should have known that she wouldn't be able to sleep or eat until she heard the sound of his voice or the feel of his lips on her clit.

They'd been together three years. It was timeout for all the bullshit, yet McKinley loved him too much to let him go. Wondering if she'd somehow missed his call, McKinley walked across the room and picked up her phone. The words *One Missed Call* were nowhere to be found on the display. Determined to get an explanation for his absence, McKinley called Jamil again, but he still wouldn't pick up the phone.

Mad as hell, McKinley decided to turn off her phone. She would show his ass. No way when he decided he wanted to be bothered with her would she make it easy for him to reach her. But as soon as she turned off her phone she wondered had she made the right decision. Determined not to second guess her decision, McKinley gathered her things and went inside her bedroom.

The entire room was stark white with accents of black and yellow. The covers on her platform bed were white and at the end of it she had a black-and-white African cloth. On both sides of her bed were mirrored nightstands. On top of the nightstands were white lamps and small vases filled with yellow roses.

Stripping down to nothing but her panties, McKinley placed on a white wife-beater and climbed into bed. She hoped that watching a little television would ease the sinking sensation in the pit of her stomach. Since it was a Friday night, there wasn't much on TV, except one of her favorite shows, E's *Fashion Police*. McKinley adored Joan Rivers and her sharp comedic timing.

Yes, the show was entertaining and even brought a smile to her face from time to time, but she couldn't help feeling like with each breath she took she was drowning. After McKinley watched *Fashion Police* and TLC's *Four Weddings* and *Say Yes to the Dress: Big Bliss,* she unknowingly drifted off to sleep. It was almost four o'clock when the sound of Jamil's heavy footsteps woke her up. McKinley opened her eyes slowly as Jamil climbed into bed and lay behind her.

"You woke?" he asked, wrapping his arm around her waist.

McKinley could smell the scent of liquor on his breath.

"I am now," she replied dryly.

"You mad at me?" Jamil kissed the back of her neck.

"What you think?" she spat sarcastically.

"My bad, man. I got caught up."

"Caught up doing what? You know I had plans for us to do something tonight."

Jamil didn't answer.

"Uh hello?" she said, annoyed.

After still not getting a reply, McKinley looked over her shoulder and found Jamil with his head against the pillow asleep.

You have got to be fuckin' kiddin' me, she thought. "Wake

yo' ass up!" She pushed his arm with brute force.

Jamil snapped his eyes opened. "I'm up! I'm up!"

"No, you're not. Yo' ass was asleep."

"No, I wasn't. I swear to God I'm up."

"What I say then?" McKinley quipped.

"Babe, I'm listening. Just give me a minute. I'm fucked up right now," Jamil said, looking like he was about to throw up.

"Get away from me." McKinley jerked her arm away.

"Stop!" Jamil demanded, pulling her back into him.

"No." McKinley elbowed him. "You get on my nerves with this shit. Where were you tonight?"

"No, the question is why the fuck you have yo' phone off?" Jamil countered.

"No way are you gon' try and flip this shit around on me," McKinley said, flabbergasted. "You played me tonight."

"I love how you try to act all innocent and shit." Jamil turned her over onto her back and lay on top of her. "Answer the fuckin' question. Why was your phone off?"

"'Cause I wanted it off, that's why," McKinley spat back, trying her best to hide how bad she wanted him.

Words couldn't describe how fine Jamil was. Just the sight of him turned her on. He and Chad Ochocinco could've been twins. Jamil's skin was the color of hot cocoa on a cold winter's day and he rocked a bald head like no other. His eyes were shaped like oval shaped diamonds and his full lips and goatee drew her in every time she looked at his face. His athletic build made her and every other woman on planet Earth mouths water.

Jamil was a bad boy with a capital B. He owned and operated a construction company, but his main source of income came from selling heroin. McKinley knew that his occupation was dangerous and could one day put her in jeopardy, but to be his girl, that was the risk she was willing to take.

"What, you had some nigga over here or something?" He mean mugged her.

"Please." McKinley rolled her eyes.

"Don't make me fuck you up, McKinley," Jamil warned.

"Whatever," she huffed.

"You can stop with the tough girl act now. I said I was sorry." Jamil kissed her lightly on the mouth.

"Just go 'head, Jamil." McKinley pushed him back.

"You don't mean that." He kissed her again more forcefully.

"Yes, I do. You gon' stop doing me like this," she protested with her mouth while spreading her legs wider.

"I said I was sorry." Jamil tenderly kissed her neck.

"No, you're not." McKinley closed her eyes.

Jamil's tongue was wreaking havoc on her neck.

"You know I love you," he whispered, pushing her tank top up.

McKinley's skin smelled like cotton candy. He had to taste her. Her exposed breasts aroused him. Jamil planted soft kisses all over McKinley's collarbone and chest until his lips met her hardened nipples.

"You forgive me?" he asked, making her melt.

McKinley clutched her pelvis tight and released a soft moan. She loved it when Jamil's wet tongue flickered across her nipples. It was the one thing that made her instantly wet. Jamil took both of her supple breasts into his hands and pressed them together. The sight reminded him of two water balloons.

Then he took his tongue and ran it back and forth across each of her breasts until she couldn't take it anymore. Realizing he had her right where he wanted her, Jamil proceeded further down. McKinley watched in sheer delight, wondering what his next move would be. Yes, she could've put up a better fight, but having sex with Jamil was her kryptonite and he used it against her every time.

His dick game constantly had her in a tailspin. Every day that passed, she yearned for it more and more. Gripping her thick thighs, Jamil pushed them both back. McKinley's knees almost touched her chest. McKinley knew she was in big trouble. When Jamil went low, he'd stay there for hours.

"You still don't forgive me?" He gazed up at her with lust in his eyes.

"Uh ah." McKinley shook her head, giving him a sly grin.

"Okay." Jamil nodded.

Then without warning, he dove headfirst into the lips of her pussy. There wasn't any slow build up. Jamil went at it as if it was the very last time he'd get to taste her.

"Oh, my God," McKinley moaned, arching her head back.

All she could feel was Jamil's tongue running feverishly over her pussy.

"You forgive me?" Jamil asked, never once stopping.

"Nooooooo." McKinley clutched the sheets.

Without showing any mercy, Jamil took his fingers and opened up the lips of her pussy. McKinley's pretty pink clit was only inches away from his wet tongue. But before he gave her another oral education, Jamil massaged her pussy with his hand. Then he took two of his fingers and dipped them deep into her honey pot. McKinley was dizzy. The in-and-out motion of his fingers, plus the sensation of his tongue circling around her clit was spellbinding.

"You still don't forgive me?" Jamil questioned, sucking anxiously on her clit.

"Nooooooo." McKinley's legs began to shake.

Fed up with playing games, Jamil got up on his knees and unzipped his jeans. Lying on top of her, he kissed her mouth passionately. As their tongues swirled around each other, Jamil stuck the tip of his dick into McKinley's pussy. The sheer force and girth of his manhood caused her eyes to fly open.

"You forgive me now, don't you?" Jamil grinded his dick in a circular motion.

"Yes, I forgive you, Daddy. I forgive you."

"Lately I've been feelin'
like you're taking me for
granted."

Brandy

"Apart"

Higig from the night before, McKinley put the finishing touches on the breakfast she'd prepared for Jamil— French toast, two hard fried eggs, ham, Jimmy Dean sausage links, grits, sliced strawberries and a cup of freshly squeezed orange juice. With everything hot and ready to go, McKinley placed his plate on a wooden serving tray and headed back to her bedroom.

"Babe," she called out to him. "Babe." She nudged him with her knee, causing him to stir in his sleep. "Babe."

"Huh?" Jamil groaned.

"Wake up." McKinley nudged him once more.

This time Jamil opened his eyes.

"What's up?" He turned over.

"I made breakfast." McKinley smiled gleefully.

"Word?" He squinted his eyes and sat up.

"Yeah." She handed him a napkin. "Oh, and since I wasn't able to give you your gift last night, here." McKinley handed him a gift box that fit into the palm of his hand.

Jamil ripped off the gift wrap, opened the box and found a Frank Muller watch with the words, *With you time stands still,* engraved on the inside of the band.

"Thanks, babe." He leaned forward and gave McKinley a quick peck on the lips.

"You really like it?" she asked, hopeful.

"Yeah." Jamil closed the box and placed it beside him on

the bed.

McKinley watched him silently. It seemed to her that he was more into the breakfast than he was the gift she'd spent weeks getting customized.

"You got some more syrup?" Jamil asked, stuffing his mouth with sausage.

"Yeah, there's some in the kitchen. You want me to get you some more?" McKinley asked, trying to hide her discontent.

"Would you please?" Jamil took a gulp of orange juice from his cup.

McKinley got up and walked to the kitchen, wondering if he could see the sadness that was so clearly written all over her face.

"Ay, what time is it?" Jamil yelled.

"Nine-thirty," McKinley said with the syrup in her hand.

"Oh shit. I gotta go." Jamil removed the tray from his lap and began to put on his jeans.

"Where you going? You haven't even finished your food yet," McKinley said, feeling her temperature rise.

"I got something I need to take care of." Jamil zipped up his jeans.

"Like, you're fuckin' wit' me, right?" McKinley folded her arms across her chest.

"No." Jamil pulled his shirt on over his head.

"Okay, it's bad enough you played me last night. Now

you're gettin' ready to play me again?"

"It's too early in the morning, McKinley. Don't start that shit." Jamil placed on the watch he wore last night.

"What shit?" McKinley scrunched up her face.

"All that fuckin' complaining. Let me go take care of this and I'll get up wit' you later." Jamil kissed her on the cheek.

McKinley stood motionless. She wanted to say more, but it was useless. Jamil was already out the door. Fuming, she walked over to the bed and picked up the tray of food when she noticed his gift sitting on the bed. *Inconsiderate bastard*, she hissed inwardly, stomping toward the kitchen. McKinley was so mad that she emptied the entire tray of food, including the dishes, into the trash.

She really didn't know how much more of Jamil's insensitive attitude she could take. The shit was getting old and fast. She deserved to be treated like a queen. Yes, Jamil provided her with a lavish lifestyle that she wouldn't be able to maintain without his assistance. But all of the money in the world couldn't buy happiness and peace of mind. McKinley ran her hand through her long black hair as her house phone began to ring. Hoping that it was Jamil calling to say that he was sorry, she raced over to the phone.

To her dismay, it was her mother. McKinley rolled her eyes and let out a breath of air. She really wasn't in the mood to talk to her. Every time they talked their conversation somehow steered into how foolish she was for dropping her life back in St. Louis to be with a man whom she barely knew and who wasn't, in her mother's words, worth shit.

But what her mother didn't and couldn't understand was that from the moment they met, McKinley fell head over heels in love. She'd met Jamil while on vacation in Miami with her girlfriends. After spending every waking moment together, when it was time for her to leave, the two couldn't bear to part. They'd had a whirlwind romance that neither wanted to end.

Everyone, including her mother and friends, told her she was crazy for jumping into a relationship with a man she barely knew and for giving up her job as an underwriter to stay in a city where she knew no one. But McKinley didn't care. She was a sucker for love at first sight, so when Jamil promised her the world she believed him. Deciding she'd talk to her mother later, McKinley let her voicemail pick up the call. Just as she was about to go back to her bedroom and sulk, the phone rang again.

"C'mon, Ma. What is it?" McKinley whined, looking at the caller ID. But it wasn't her mother calling; it was her BFF of three years, Kristen, who lived two floors down.

After moving into the building, McKinley and Kristen became instant friends. They both had a shared love for designer frocks, reality television and good food. Plus, Kristen's boyfriend and Jamil ran in the same circle, so Kristen understood the trials and tribulations of dating a man who was not only wealthy, but full of drama.

"Hello?" McKinley answered the phone.

"Whaaaaat? I can't believe yo' ass up this time of the morning."

"Shut up." McKinley chuckled, sitting down on the couch.

"I just saw your nigga leave as I was coming in."

"It's only nine-fifteen, Kristen. Where in the hell have you been already?"

"While yo' ass was in the bed, fuckin' and suckin', I went to the gym and then to the grocery store. Something you know nothin' about," Kristen said with a laugh.

"You got that right," McKinley responded unenthusiastically.

"What's wrong wit' you?" Kristen asked, hearing the sound of sadness in her voice.

"Nothin'." McKinley sighed.

"McKinley, this is me. I know when there's something wrong wit' you. What has Jamil done now?"

"Girl, he just gets on my nerve." McKinley rolled her eyes. "You know I planned that whole big ta-da for his birthday, and do you know he didn't even bother to show up? I sat in that restaurant for damn near an hour and a half like a goddamn dummy before I finally said fuck it and went home."

"So what was his excuse for not showing up?" Kristen

asked, unlocking the door to her apartment.

"Now that I think about it, he never really gave me an explanation," McKinley replied, having what Oprah Winfrey called an "aha moment."

"Now that I think about it, instead of him tellin' me where he was, that muthafucka turned the shit around on me and went off on me for turning my phone off."

"Tricky bastard," Kristen grinned.

"I can't believe that nigga got over on me again," McKinley replied in disbelief.

"Niggas," Kristen said, putting up her groceries. "Can't live with 'em, can't live without 'em."

"I'm just tired of him treating me like this. He's just so fuckin' insensitive."

"Aren't all men?" Kristen joked.

"I guess you have a point," McKinley agreed.

"Look, girl," Kristen stopped dead in her tracks. "Fuck Jamil. If he wanna act a fool let him. Tony ass on some bullshit too, but you think I'm over here on suicide watch? No. I'm doin' me 'cause guess what? Ain't none of this shit new. We know how these niggas are and we're both choosing to stay, so why continue to cry and whine every time they do something fucked up? You think they trippin' off us right now? No. So let's take a page from their book and not trip off they ass either."

"You're right." McKinley let out a much-needed breath.

She wanted to be strong like Kristen, but deep down inside she knew thoughts of Jamil would control her mind for the rest of the day. The shit was sickening. It was like she lived and breathed him.

"Check it. How about we have a 'I'm Doin' Me Day'? We're gonna get dressed, get our nails and feet done, grab lunch, then go shoppin'. And to finish out our 'I'm Doin' Me Day' we'll put on our flyest outfits and head to Mansion tonight. What do you say?" Kristen exclaimed. "And I'm not takin' no for an answer," she added.

"Well, I guess that's a yes then." McKinley laughed.

"Oh, and if Tony or Jamil call we have to promise not to pick up the phone."

"Now you reaching," McKinley countered.

"Quit being a punk. Besides, how many times have you called Jamil and he didn't answer your calls? Case in point, last night on his birthday. One day of giving that nigga yo' ass to kiss won't hurt. If anything, it'll put a fire under his ass and make him act right for a change. And another thing—"

McKinley caved in. "Okay, okay, okay. I swear, you should've went to law school 'cause yo' ass can talk a mutha-fucka into anything."

"I'll take that as a compliment," Kristen replied. "Now be ready by eleven."

"A'ight."

"And don't take all day, McKinley. You got almost two hours to get ready," Kristen stressed.

"Okay, heffa."

"Whatever, bitch, meet me in the lobby at eleven," Kristen said before hanging up.

"Deuces."

XoXo

"I swear yo' ass gon' be late for your own funeral," Kristen said, pulling out of the parking lot of her and McKinley's building.

"You can't rush perfection." McKinley looked in the rearview mirror and applied another coat of pink Chanel lip gloss.

"Bitch, you look a'ight." Kristen pushed the passenger's visor mirror up in its appropriate position, snapping it closed.

"Uh." McKinley screwed up her face. "Don't be a hater."

"Chile, please. I'm far from a hater. I mean, have you taken a good look at me lately? I'm the shit, bitch."

"Whatever. You look a'ight, but please believe you ain't flyer than me." McKinley grinned as the wind whipped through their hair.

McKinley would never admit it to Kristen, because she was so vain, but Kristen was supermodel gorgeous. She was tall and statuesque with a sepia skin tone. Kristen rocked her hair in a super cute bob with blunt bangs. Kristen had a full bust and plump ass to fill out her clothes.

"So where are we going?" McKinley inquired. "'Cause it's like ninety-five degrees outside and I'm not tryin' to be out in the heat. 'Cause you know with the kinda hair I got my shit gon' be lookin' like Chaka Khan's in a matter of seconds. And I did not spend a half an hour flat ironing my hair for nothin'.'"

"Now I see why Jamil stood you up, 'cause you's one complaining bitch." Kristen grimaced.

"Just answer the question, trick," McKinley snapped.

"We're going to Blush to get our mani-pedis, lil' nosy-ass girl."

"Cool, 'cause I wanna change my color." McKinley looked down at her nails as her cell phone started to ring. "Uh ah," McKinley snarled.

"What?" Kristen looked over.

"Jamil's callin' me."

"You bet' not answer that phone," Kristen warned.

"I'm not." McKinley slid her phone back inside her purse. "Like you said, I'm doin' me today." She smiled brightly.

"She put up wit' it 'cause she know that dick be dynamite."

Masspike Miles featuring Rick Ross

"Nasty"

After being fully pampered and shopping until her wallet screamed "STOOOOOOOOOOOOP," McKinley returned home. She couldn't wait to dump her things out on the bed and get dolled up for a night on the town with her girl. Kristen had been right, their day of doin' them was empowering. It felt good not to sit in the house and sulk over Jamil's latest disappointment.

He'd been blowin' up her cell phone non-stop, but McKinley never once caved in and answered the phone. It felt good to have him wondering where she was and what she was doing. McKinley dug inside her Birkin bag and pulled out her key to unlock the door. As soon as she stepped across the threshold, she dropped her bags and screamed.

"Where the fuck you been?" Jamil barked, sitting on the couch.

"Boy, you scared the shit outta me." McKinley held her chest.

"Fuck all of that. Answer the question. Where you been?"

"Out. Why?" McKinley curled her upper lip and bent over to pick up her bags.

"You know why. Why the fuck you ain't been answering my calls?"

"The same reason you didn't answer mine last night," McKinley shot back sarcastically.

"Oh, now you on some ole other shit. Why everything gotta

be a game wit' you? I'm gettin' real sick of you not answering my calls 'cause you call yo'self being mad. How about I get that muthafucka turned off then, since you don't like answering it. Then we can just go our separate ways. You can take yo' ass back to St. Louis. 'Cause you ain't about to play me like I'm some bitch-ass nigga," Jamil barked.

"Really, Jamil?" McKinley cocked her head to the side, outdone by his statement. "Don't you think you're carrying on a bit?"

"No."

"Well, why is it every time I do something you don't like you wanna call it quits?"

"Look, this is my life. Anything could've happened to me and you wouldn't have known. All because you wanna play tit for tat."

McKinley hated to admit it, but Jamil had a point.

"You know what? You're right. I just feel like sometimes you don't care," she admitted.

"If I didn't care I wouldn't be here. Look," he waved his hand. "I'm tired of talkin'. Come here." He beckoned for her to sit on his lap.

McKinley sauntered over to Jamil, trying her best not to smile.

"I love you." He stared deep into her eyes. "Don't shit else matter."

"I know, it's just that—"

"Shhhhhhh." Jamil cut her off by placing his index finger up to her lips. "I don't wanna talk no more. I wanna see what you got on underneath this lil bitty ass dress." He slid his hands underneath her skirt and massaged her bare ass. "Aww, yeah?" He smiled, surprised. "Yo' ass really in trouble now. Give me a kiss," Jamil demanded.

McKinley placed her hands on the side of his face and slowly kissed his lips.

"You   gon'   give   me   some?"
McKinley quickly got up. "Uh ah, Jamil, we are not gettin' ready to have sex. I promised Kristen I'd go out wit' her tonight." She got up.

He looked up at her. "So going out wit' yo' homegirl is more important than spending time wit' ya' man?"

"Here you go." McKinley groaned, tucking her hair behind her ear.

Jamil nodded his head repeatedly then unzipped his jeans. "It's cool."

He pulled out his dick and began talking to it. "You see how she doing us, man?"

This nigga is not fighting fair, McKinley thought, licking her lips.

If there were two things in life she couldn't resist, it was an end-of-the-season sale and Jamil's big, brown juicy dick.

To her it was a work of art, and to see it sticking straight up in the air like a missile, while Jamil ran his hand up and down its shaft, put her in a trance. McKinley didn't even realize that she'd taken him in her mouth until she was on her knees. She thoroughly enjoyed sucking Jamil's dick. It always seemed to glide in and out of her mouth with velvet ease.

"Fuck," Jamil groaned.

McKinley sucked his dick like a porn star. Wanting a better view, Jamil combed McKinley's hair over to the side with his fingertips and watched with pleasure as she slid her tongue from his balls up to the tip of his dick. Ready to put his thing down, Jamil said, "Come here."

McKinley straddled him and eased down slowly onto his dick.

"Damn, baby, you wet." Jamil gripped her butt cheeks and helped her bounce up and down.

"I know, baby, this dick feels so good." She whimpered as her cell phone rang.

"Mmm, hold up. Let me get that, that's Kristen." She tried reaching for her phone.

"You wasn't answering yo' phone earlier, so don't answer it now. I got this. You concentrate on riding this dick." Jamil slapped her on the ass and answered her phone.

"Are you ready?" Kristen asked, dryly.

"Yo, listen. She ain't comin'. I mean, well, she is cumming, but you get the picture." Jamil chuckled.

"Jamil," McKinley shrieked, still bouncing.

"Oh, my God! Y'all are disgusting. Bye!" Kristen hung up.

Jamil cracked a smile and hung up, too.

"You love this dick, don't you?" He slapped her ass again.

"Oooooh, yes," McKinley screamed, feeling an orgasm coming near. "Shit, babe." She rocked back and forth. "Oh, my God, this dick feels so good!"

"You finna come?" Jamil could feel a nut build in the tip of his dick.

"Yes!"

"Me, too." Jamil came without pulling out.

Calming down from her orgasmic high, McKinley stood up and plopped down onto the couch.

"That was so good, I wanna buy you a short set." She panted heavily, trying to catch her breath.

"You want something to drink?" Jamil asked, going inside the kitchen.

"Yeah, get me a bottled water, please."

Jamil quickly returned with both of their drinks.

"Thanks, baby." McKinley took a long gulp. "Whew! I needed that."

"Why don't you go get dressed, so we can go out?" Jamil asked.

"For real?" McKinley looked at him surprised.

"Yeah."

"Bet." She jumped up from the couch and raced to her bedroom.

XoXo

It was midnight when McKinley and Jamil walked hand in hand into club Mansion. Mansion was one of the premiere places to be in Miami. On any given night, you could run into a top-line celebrity like Kourtney Kardashian, Diddy or Drake. There was always a party being thrown by an A-list celeb or a one-time-only performance by your favorite artist. Being inside Mansion was like being transported into another realm. The space was humongous. More than five-hundred people could fit inside of the club.

But even with the slew of scantily clad women in the crowd, none could outshine McKinley. Homegirl was fresh to death in a colorful, multi-strand, beaded necklace, white scoop-neck oversized T-shirt with the sleeves rolled up, lime-green bandage skirt and purple Manolo Blahnik patent leather heels. Her long hair was parted down the center and flat ironed bone straight. To finish off the look, she rocked a hot pink, Valentino Noeud d'Amore clutch.

Jamil didn't look too bad either. He donned a blue jean jacket with the sleeves shrugged up. In the pocket of the jacket was a crème colored handkerchief. Underneath the jacket, he wore a blue V-neck tee. To complete his look, he sported a pair of dirty wash jeans and brown leather combat boots. McKinley and Jamil were such a stunning couple that partygoers couldn't help but stop and stare as they walked by. As McKinley strutted up the steps to the VIP area, she spotted Kristen on the dance floor, dancing as if she didn't have a care in the world.

"Hold up, babe. I see Kristen. Let me go say hi to her," McKinley said in mid-stride.

"A'ight. Tell her to come up in VIP wit' us," Jamil suggested.

"Okay," McKinley said, turning around.

The crowd on the dance floor was so thick that it took McKinley almost five minutes to get to Kristen. Sleigh Bells' "Infinity Guitar" was blasting through the speakers and Kristen was all into the beat.

"You look cute," McKinley yelled into her ear over the loud music.

Kristen spun around. "Bitch!" She opened her arms wide and hugged McKinley. "What are you doing here? I thought you were standing me up for yo' nigga?"

"I technically did. He's upstairs in VIP. You mad at me?" McKinley poked out her bottom lip.

"You fake, but whatever." Kristen waved her off.

"C'mon, you wanna come upstairs wit' us?"

"What, so I can be the third wheel?" Kristen cocked her

head back. "I think not."

"Girl, you know it ain't nothin' like that. C'mon." McKinley took her hand, not taking no for an answer.

To both McKinley and Kristen's surprise, when they entered the VIP area, they found Jamil and Kristen's boyfriend, Tony, smoking cigars and poppin' bottles with one another.

"Did you know he was here?" Kristen asked McKinley.

"No. I'm just as surprised as you are," McKinley responded.

Kristen stomped over to Tony. "What the hell are you doing here?"

"I knew you was gon' have yo' hot ass up in the club tonight, so I decided to pop up on you. You still mad at me?" Tony invaded Kristen's personal space.

"What you think?" Kristen replied, not backing down.

"I take that as a yes." He laughed.

"You damn right." Kristen rolled her eyes.

"Why you so damn mean? You know that shit turn me on." Tony wrapped her up in his arms.

"I can't stand you." Kristen shook her head and cracked a smile.

Happy to see her friend smiling, McKinley walked over to her man who was holding a glass of champagne for her.

Jamil held up his glass. "To us."

"To us." McKinley tapped her glass against his then took a

sip when "Wet" by Snoop Dogg came on.

"Aww shit! That's my song." She sat her glass down and started grooving.

Kristen loved the song, too, and started jamming to the song with her.

"Tell me, baby, are you wet? I just wanna get you wet." They sang the song while rolling their hips.

Jamil loved nothing more than to see McKinley lose herself within the beat of a song. McKinley could dance her ass off. Her moves were so sensual and hypnotizing. She knew how to roll her stomach and hips just like a belly dancer and pop her ass like a video vixen. Jamil watched as her round booty twirled around in circles. The skintight skirt she wore emphasized her moves and curves. The sight was too much for him to handle. It made him dizzy with lust.

McKinley looked over her shoulder at him. She could see the look of desire in his eyes. Knowing just how to turn him on, she backed her ass up on him. Jamil placed his hands on her hips and danced with her. For the rest of the night the two love birds enjoyed each other's company. They laughed, drank and danced until the wee hours of the morning.

"I'm pissed off. I want you to feel the same."

Dawn Richards

"I'm Just Sayin'"

After a long fun-filled night of grooving to their favorite Hip Hop and R&B artists and sipping on the finest liquor Mansion had to offer, McKinley and Jamil returned home. As soon as they walked through the door, Jamil stripped down and went to bed. Normally, McKinley would've gone right to bed too, but she had to clean her kitchen. The dishes from the previous morning were still in the sink and McKinley was not raised to go to bed with a dirty kitchen.

While Jamil lay underneath the covers, soaking up the central air, she stood barefoot at the kitchen sink, washing the dishes by hand. McKinley was halfway done when she heard a loud buzzing sound. Wondering where the sound was coming from, McKinley turned off the faucet and listened closely. The buzzing noise wasn't coming from the kitchen so she walked into the living room. McKinley was so focused on locating the noise that she didn't notice Jamil's Lanvin sneakers and jeans in the middle of the floor, causing her to almost trip and fall.

"I'ma kick his ass," she hissed, bending over to pick up his things.

Then she heard the buzzing sound come from his jeans.

Who in the hell is callin' him this early in the morning, she thought, holding his jeans up to her chest. Immediately, memories of Jamil's past infidelities came rushing to her mind. Yeah, she'd forgiven him for his past transgressions, but once he'd cheated on her that feeling of betrayal never went away. She knew it was wrong to snoop because when you look for trouble you usually find it, but she had to know who was calling him. Quietly, she reached into his pocket and pulled out his cell phone. The screen revealed that he had a text message from someone named T. The message read:

From: T

Where r u? I'm @ home.

Sent:

Sun, May 21, 4:37 am

Chill bumps immediately spread across McKinley's arms and legs, she was so enraged. Breathing heavily, she glanced over her shoulder to ensure the coast was clear, it was. She had to confirm that this T person was a girl, so McKinley pressed the call button and dialed the person's phone. Two rings later, a woman answered the phone. Hearing the woman's voice crushed her heart. Tears instantly formed in her eyes, but she was determined not to cry.

"Hello?" the woman said again.

McKinley didn't bother to say anything. Instead, she ended the call and went back into the kitchen. Grabbing a pin and a piece of paper, she quickly jotted down the girl's number and stashed it in one of the kitchen drawers she knew Jamil never went in. Now that she had all the ammunition she needed to

Keisha Ervin

pounce on his cheating ass, McKinley raced up the stairs and barged into their bedroom.

"Jamil!" she yelled, pushing his arm.

"What?" He screwed up his face.

"Wake up!" McKinley spat.

"What the fuck are you yellin' for?" Jamil turned over onto his side.

"Get yo' ass up!" McKinley yelled even louder.

"Yo, on the real, McKinley. I ain't in the mood for no bull-shit tonight," Jamil warned. "It's four-thirty in the morning. What the fuck do you want?" he groaned.

"Who the fuck is T?" McKinley held up his phone.

"What?" He eyed her, confused.

"Please." McKinley put her hand up as if to say pause. "Let's not play dumb. Just answer the fuckin' question. Who is T?"

"I don't know." He looked away.

"Really? Well, apparently she knows you 'cause she just sent you a text message, asking where you were at." McKinley threw his phone at him, almost hitting him in the head with it.

"You out yo' fuckin' mind?" Jamil dodged the phone and sat up. "Don't throw shit else at me, McKinley. 'Cause if I get to throwin' shit you ain't gon' like it. And what the fuck you doing going through my phone?"

"Just answer the fuckin' question! Who is T?" McKinley

shot sternly.

"A girl," Jamil replied sarcastically.

"I know she's a girl, douchebag. Who is she?"

"Since you're so fuckin' nosy. She's one of my business pot'nahs."

"Do I look that stupid to you?" McKinley placed her hand on her hip.

"Honestly, you do 'cause you always jumpin' to conclusions, assuming shit and you don't know what the hell you're talkin' about."

"What kind of business partner calls you at four o'clock in the morning? Just admit it, Jamil. You're cheating on me again, aren't you?"

"I ain't gotta put up with this shit." He flung his legs out of the bed and got up.

"Where you think you going?" She eyed him in disbelief.

"Where it look like I'm going? Home!" He shot over his shoulder.

"Really, Jamil? So you just gon' leave? You not gon' even tell me the truth?" McKinley followed him down the stairs.

"I have told you the truth. It's up to you to believe it. And where the fuck are my clothes?" He searched the first floor.

"In the kitchen." McKinley folded her arms across her chest.

"Why are my clothes in the kitchen?" Jamil barked.

"'Cause I took 'em in there. That's why."

"So you just going through all of my shit, huh?" Jamil smirked, placing on his jeans.

"Whatever," McKinley rolled her eyes. "I don't see shit funny."

"You's a fuckin' trip, you know that? You invade my privacy and got the nerve to have an attitude?"

"You damn right, I got an attitude. You got bitches callin' yo' phone and then gon' sit up here and lie to my face about it. Are you crazy?"

"You can believe what you wanna believe. I ain't gotta explain myself to you." Jamil took his car keys out of his pocket.

"So you seriously gettin' ready to leave?" McKinley said, distraught. She couldn't believe that he wouldn't own up to the fact that he'd been caught. Instead, like always, he flipped the situation around and made her feel like the guilty party.

"Yeah, I am," he confirmed. "Until you can learn how to trust me, I don't think we need to be wit' each other."

"So not only are you leaving, but you're breaking up with me?" McKinley said stunned.

"I mean, what else you want me to do? You don't trust me."

"And you've given me every reason under the sun not to. All you do is lie."

"Whatever, man. I'll holla at you later." Jamil placed his hand on the knob.

"Are you serious right now?" McKinley began to cry.

She didn't understand how he could be upset when he was the one who'd done wrong.

"I'll call you tomorrow or something." He opened the door and left.

McKinley thought about running after him, but running after him would only make her feel stupid in the end. When Jamil was on his soapbox, he wouldn't come down until he had McKinley down on her knees or until he had no other choice but to confess. It was sad, but that was how he was. McKinley just had to figure out what her next move would be. She couldn't let another day go by without knowing where she really stood with Jamil.

XoXo

McKinley knocked on Kristen's door the following morning. "Code 10! Code 10! We got a man-down situation."

"What the hell is going on?" Kristen opened up the door and let McKinley in.

"I'm sorry, were you asleep?" McKinley asked, noticing she had on a robe.

"No, just gettin' my bed rocked," Kristen said out of the side of her mouth.

"Oh, my bad, is Tony here?" McKinley whispered back.

"Yeah, I am." He came out of the back, pulling his T-shirt

on over his head.

"You gettin' ready to leave?" Kristen asked disappointed.

"Yeah, I'ma shake, but I'll be back in a couple of hours." He kissed her on the forehead. "I love you."

"I love you, too." Kristen poked out her bottom lip.

"Bye, Tony." McKinley waved.

"Stay up, McKinley." He walked out of the door.

"Now, what the hell is the emergency, cockblocker?" Kristen tightened her robe.

"You will not believe what happened last night." McKinley barged into Kristen's kitchen and started rummaging through her cabinets. "You got any saltines? I need something to settle my stomach." McKinley looked over her shoulder.

"Yeah, in the cabinet on your left, and please tell me you're not pregnant." Kristen followed her into the kitchen.

"Hell no. I've been up drinkin' and thinkin'."

"Why?" Kristen sat on top of the counter.

"Some girl named T texted Jamil last night when we got home from the club."

"Get outta here." Kristen crossed her legs.

"Yes, and when I confronted him about it, he gon' lie and say she one of his 'business pot'nahs'." McKinley made air quotes with her fingers. "Then he got an attitude wit' me."

"Ain't that what they always do?" Kristen chuckled.

"I know he lying though."

"Uh, duh." Kristen rolled her neck. "Yeah, that nigga lyin'. You think he just gon' come out and say, yeah I'm stickin' my dick in her?"

"Well, we gettin' ready to find out for sure." McKinley went into her back pocket and pulled out a piece of paper. "'Cause you gettin' ready to call her."

"You say what now?" Kristen cocked her head back.

"Please, Kristen." McKinley clasped her hands together. "I'm too emotional to talk to her, and plus, I might cuss her out if she step outta line."

"And what the hell you think I'ma do?"

"C'mon, Kristen. I would do it for you. Hell, I *have* done it for you."

"Give me the goddamn number." Kristen snatched the piece of paper from McKinley's hand.

"Thank you," McKinley smiled.

Kristen grabbed the cordless phone and dialed the girl's number, but not before pressing *67, and putting the call on speakerphone.

"Hello?"

"Hi, may I speak to T?" Kristen asked sweetly.

"Who is this?" the woman asked.

"This is McKinley, Jamil's girlfriend."

"Uh, huh?" the girl said unfazed.

"Is this T?" Kristen asked again.

"Yeah, this me," T answered with an attitude.

"Listen, I'm not callin' you to argue or anything like that. I just wanted to know if you and Jamil messing around?"

McKinley crossed her fingers and prayed to God that the girl's answer would be no.

"I think you need to ask Jamil that," T remarked dryly.

"So I take that as a yes," Kristen responded.

"Like I said, you need to ask your man that question," T replied before hanging up.

"Bitch," Kristen spat, hanging up as well. "Well, I guess you got your answer." She gave McKinley a sad face.

Heartbroken, McKinley placed down the saltines and stood paralyzed. She felt so stupid for even giving Jamil the benefit of the doubt. He didn't deserve it, just like he didn't deserve her.

"So what are you going to do?" Kristen asked.

"I'ma fuck his ass up. That's what I'ma do." McKinley pulled out her cell phone and called him.

"What's up?" Jamil answered the phone with a smile. He just knew that McKinley was calling him to apologize.

"Come get your shit," McKinley hissed.

"What?" Jamil said, caught off guard.

"You heard me. Come get your shit. I am done fuckin' wit' you. You've been cheating on me this whole time with that bitch."

"You still on that? I told you I wasn't doing nothin'," Jamil replied mildly.

"Just stop lying. I talked to the girl, Jamil."

"You did what?" His voice went up an octave.

"Yeah, that's right. I talked to her and she told me everything that I needed to know, so come get your shit 'cause I'm done." McKinley pressed the *End* button.

As soon as she hung up, Jamil called her right back, but she didn't even bother to pick up.

"You gon' be okay, friend?" Kristen asked concerned.

"I will be once I get his ass out of my life. Look, let me go back up to my apartment. I'm sure he's on his way over there."

"Okay." Kristen hopped down from the counter. "Call me if you need me."

"I will." McKinley left out and boarded the elevator.

By the time she reached her apartment, Jamil had called her over ten times. On a mission to rid herself of him, McKinley stormed into her place and began collecting all of his things. She'd successfully thrown his underwear and socks and half of his clothes down the stairs when he came walking through the door.

"McKinley," he called out for her.

"I don't wanna hear shit you got to say, Jamil. Just get your shit and go." She threw one of his coats over the rail.

"Have you lost yo' mind? Stop throwing my shit," he

yelled from the first floor.

"Fuck you," McKinley shouted back.

"Yo, will you let me explain?" He dodged a boot that was being thrown at his head then ran up the steps.

"Explain what? That you're a fuckin' lyin' ass piece of shit? I can't believe you've been cheating on me again. Here I was thinkin' we were doing better, but no, you don't give a fuck about me. You gon' continue to do you."

"I'm tellin' you I didn't cheat on you." Jamil got into her face and held her by the arms.

"Let me go, Jamil." McKinley closed her eyes.

"No. Not until you listen to me."

"I don't wanna hear shit you got to say. All I wanna see is your back walking out the door, straight up."

"So you not gon' let me tell you what happened?"

"What about "I'm done fuckin' wit' you" don't you understand? It's over. Just get your shit and go."

"That's really how you feel?" Jamil said, taken aback by her persistence.

"Yeah."

"Well, fuck you then." He let her go.

"Fuck me?" McKinley's eyes grew wide. "Fuck me?" Her lips trembled. "Nigga, fuck you," she spat as he walked down the steps and out the door.

XoXo

Around ten o'clock that night, McKinley sat in bed watching the Showtime hit *Shameless*. She had a bowl of buttered popcorn and a Mountain Dew slush to wash it down. She'd fully made it up in her mind that she and Jamil were done for good. She'd had enough of being tortured by his lies. It was time for her to take a cue from Kristen and the singer Fantasia and start doing her.

If she was going to be miserable, then she'd much rather be miserable by herself. Laughing, she reached inside the bowl and pulled out a handful of popcorn when she received a text message from Jamil. McKinley rolled her eyes and viewed it.

From: Jamil

I'm sorry

Sent:

Sun, May 21, 10:22 pm

"You're sorry all right." She erased the message and threw her phone down.

A few minutes later, he sent her another message.

From: Jamil

Baby, please 4give me. You know I can't live without u.

Sent:

Sun, May 21, 10:26 pm

"He is so whack." She smirked when he texted her again.

From: Jamil

C'mon, ma, don't do this. U know ur my baby. I luv u.

Sent:

Sun, May 21, 10:28 pm

McKinley erased the message and continued to ignore him when he sent another message.

From: Jamil

Can I please come talk 2 u?

Sent:

Sun, May 21, 10:31 pm

McKinley inhaled deeply. She couldn't front, she liked to see Jamil beg. It made her feel like she was the one in charge. Plus, she'd wanted to hear from him anyway. It would've killed her if he hadn't tried reaching out to her, so she texted him back.

To: Jamil

Yeah

Sent:

Sun, May 21, 10:39 pm

A minute hadn't even gone by before she heard him enter the house.

"This muthafucka been standing outside this whole time," she said out loud to herself.

Jamil came up the stairs and stood in the doorway of their bedroom with his hands inside his pockets and stared at her.

He spoke softly. "What's up?"

"You tell me." McKinley cocked her head to the side.

"You know I love you like a fat kid love cake," he joked, making her laugh.

"Whatever, Jamil."

"Real talk, you and I are good together; you know that, don't you?"

"Yeah, I know it." She placed her head down.

"You love me?"

"No." She bit the inside of her bottom lip.

"You know I can always tell when you're lying 'cause you bite the inside of your lip." Jamil came toward her and kissed her on the lips.

"Shut up." McKinley pushed him away.

"You gotta believe me, baby. I ain't fuckin' wit' nobody, but you."

"Well, why would she tell me to ask you if y'all mess around then?"

"I don't know. All I know is that I love you." Jamil took her into his arms.

"Jamil, I can't take too much more of this." McKinley's voice shook slightly.

"I know, baby, I know."

"*No more tryin', tired of feelin' like I'm the only one dyin'.*"

Dawn Richards

"*I'm Just Sayin'*"

A fter a couple of blissful weeks together, McKinley awoke, expecting to see Jamil's face, but instead found that she was alone.

"I know that muthafucka didn't leave without sayin' nothin'." She snatched the covers off of her and got up.

Dressed in one of Jamil's oversized T-shirts, she searched the second floor of her apartment until she found him in the spare bedroom that she'd converted into an office/sitting room. There he was sitting on the couch with his feet propped up on a footstool, playing Call of Duty.

"I was gettin' ready to say." McKinley let out a sigh of relief.

He quickly looked up at her. "Say what?"

"Nothin'." McKinley went and sat on the arm of the couch. "How long have you been up?"

"Umm . . . almost two hours." Jamil focused in on the game.

"Why didn't you wake me?"

"'Cause I knew you were tired." He pressed the *A* button on the controller repeatedly.

"So you've been up almost two hours and the only thing you've accomplished is playing this dumb video game? Like really, Jamil? You couldn't have found something more productive to do with your time?"

"You complain entirely too much. If complaining was

against the law you'd go to jail," he joked.

"Excuse you. I am not a complainer."

"Yeah, you are. How about instead of running your mouth all the time, you open up your eyes and take a look around before you get to judging."

"What have you done?" McKinley's face lit up with a smile.

"Go and see," Jamil said, putting the game on pause.

Before he knew it, McKinley was gone. If there was one thing on earth that McKinley loved, more than she loved Chanel, was a good surprise. McKinley raced down the steps and found that the dining room table had been completely set and was filled with every delectable breakfast food you could imagine.

"Oh, my God," she gushed, inching toward the table.

Jamil had outdone himself. There were pancakes, French toast, waffles, grits, eggs, bacon, sausage, ham, hash browns, toast and a choice of orange juice, coffee or water. But what stood out the most was the small, square, velvet box that sat directly in the center of the table amongst all of the food. McKinley couldn't believe her eyes. *I swear, if this is a joke I'ma kill 'em,* she thought, picking up the box. Holding her breath, McKinley opened the box. Inside was a flawless, 5-carat, canary yellow, Harry Winston, square-cut diamond. The sight of the ring and the meaning behind it brought tears to her eyes.

"Baby," Jamil said from behind on one knee.

"Huh?" McKinley spun around swiftly.

"I know that we've had our ups and downs, but I love you and I don't wanna spend my life with anyone else, but you. Will you marry me?"

"Are you kidding me? Yes!" McKinley clasped her hands together and jumped up and down.

Jamil grinned. "Give me your hand."

McKinley extended her left hand and watched in awe as Jamil placed the ring on her finger. "It's beautiful."

"You're beautiful." Jamil kissed the outside of her hand and stood up.

"I can't believe this is happening." McKinley wrapped her arms around Jamil's neck and squeezed him tight.

"I don't see why. You know that I love you."

"I know." She released her arms from around him and stepped back.

"It's just that—" She tried to speak, but couldn't because tears had started to rise in her throat.

"Stop." Jamil pulled her back into his embrace. "I know that things between us ain't always been good and that's mostly because of me. But on everything, I love you. I ain't on that shit no more. I'ma do right by you. Plus, I think it's time we start having some lil mini-me's runnin' around here." He picked her up in his arms and swung her around.

"You are crazy." McKinley giggled, feeling like she was about to burst from happiness.

Finally, everything she'd wished for was coming true. She'd prayed for years that this day would come. Jamil was the love of her life. Yes, he came with flaws, but who didn't? He loved her and she loved him. Anything her heart desired, he provided. Yes, because he was a drug dealer, she often found herself at home alone, but to know that she would now have him to herself for the rest of her life was good enough for her.

"You love me?" Jamil placed her down and planted a deep kiss on her lips.

"Of course."

"Well, come show me how much then." He took her hand and led her back into the bedroom.

After spending the rest of the morning in bed, making love, McKinley fell asleep in Jamil's arms.

Around one o'clock that afternoon, McKinley opened her eyes once again to find herself in bed alone, except this time when she went searching the house for Jamil he was nowhere to be found. She did, however, find the living room filled with over five different bouquets of flowers.

"Awwwwwwwwww." McKinley leaned over and inhaled the potent scent. "My day is just getting better and better." She gleamed with delight.

Seeing the sea of flowers warmed her heart. The gesture

made her feel so special. She had to call Jamil to thank him. Using the cordless phone in the kitchen, she dialed his number. McKinley let the phone ring until his voicemail picked up.

"Hey, babe, thank you for the flowers. They're beautiful. I love them. I wish you would've told me you were leaving, but it's cool. I love you anyway. Just call me when you get this message."

XoXo

Distraught, McKinley paced back and forth across her living room floor in a purple maxi dress. Days had gone by and she hadn't heard from Jamil. She'd called him so much, the tips of her fingers were sore. Each time the phone would just ring and then go to voicemail. Sometimes her calls were forwarded to voicemail. She'd even tried texting him, but nothing worked. Jamil just wouldn't pick up the phone.

McKinley felt as if she'd been sucker-punched. It never failed, every time she got comfortable and made herself believe that things between them would be different, he always revealed his true self. She was so over the sleepless nights, broken promises, excuses and lame-ass apologies that came behind the whack-ass excuses. She desperately wanted to believe that the Jamil, who looked her in the eyes and confessed his undying love, sang to her at night and even broke down in tears over her was the real him. But his actions kept showing her that he was an unreliable, selfish liar. He would continue to take her through unnecessary drama for the simple fact that he could. McKinley just prayed that he wasn't with another chick. She couldn't go through that kind of pain again.

"Has he ever done anything like this before?" Kristen asked, sitting on the couch Indian style.

"No." McKinley continued to pace the room. "The longest we've ever gone without speaking is maybe two days, but that's when we're mad at each other."

"Does he have a house phone at his apartment?"

"No, just his cell." McKinley massaged her forehead.

"You don't know any of his friends' numbers, so you can call and see if they've talked to him?" Kristen quizzed.

"No, and besides, Jamil would kill me if I called his friends lookin' for him," McKinley said, flushing in distress.

"Mmm." Kristen arched her eyebrow, shocked by her answer. "Well, I don't know, friend." She picked up the bag of hot popcorn and resumed eating.

Not the one to give up, McKinley went to her contacts on her cell phone and pressed Jamil's name. After two rings she was forwarded to voicemail again.

"Oh, my God!" She mashed down the *End* button. "Like really? This nigga is straight up sending me to voicemail."

"Wow." Kristen shook her head.

"Like, I swear to God I'ma fuck him up when I see him,"

McKinley fumed. "I mean, like who proposes to someone then disappears for four days?"

"Jamil." Kristen couldn't help but laugh.

McKinley stopped mid-stride and glared at her. "Word?" She shot Kristen a look that could kill.

"I'm sorry. You left yourself wide open for that one. Look," Kristen put down the bag of popcorn, "on the real, try callin' him one more time and if he doesn't answer then fuck it. Don't call his ass no more." She flicked her wrist.

"That's easier said than done," McKinley retorted indignantly. "This ain't just some nigga. This is the man I've been wit' for the last three years of my life. I can't just sit back not knowing whether he's dead or alive. What if something happened to him? Then what?" She threw her hands up in the air.

"You don't know his mama's number? I mean damn," Kristen responded, not knowing what else to do.

"No, they don't speak." McKinley ran her hands down her face.

"Then call him again, stalker." Kristen rolled her eyes and took a sip of her soda.

McKinley eagerly dialed Jamil's number, praying this time he would answer.

"Hello?" A little boy answered the phone.

"Uhhhhhhhhhhhhhhhhh." McKinley took the phone away from her ear to make sure she'd dialed the right number. "Is

Jamil there?"

"This is me," the little boy replied, cheerfully.

"No, sweetie, I'm looking for Jamil," McKinley repeated, but in a louder tone as if the boy was deaf.

"This is me, silly lady." The boy chuckled.

"Ummm," McKinley looked at Kristen confused, "is your daddy there?" she probed.

"Are you serious?" Kristen mouthed.

"Yeah. You wanna talk to him? 'Cause he makin' me a peanut butter and jelly sandwich right now," the boy said.

"Yes. Can you put him on the phone?" McKinley asked, feeling faint.

"Okay." The boy put down the phone. "Daddy. Telephone."

"What?" McKinley swore she heard Jamil say in the background.

The next thing she knew the phone went dead and she was left with silence. Shocked by what had just taken place, she stood paralyzed in the center of the floor.

"What happened?" Kristen asked, genuinely concerned.

Anxiety was written all over McKinley's face. "Some lil boy answered the phone," McKinley responded in a daze, "and he said that his name was Jamil. I asked him to put his daddy on the phone and the boy said okay. Then the boy called out for his daddy, and I swear, Kristen, I heard Jamil say 'what' in the background." Her eyes bucked.

"Hell naw," Kristen said, dumbfounded. "So you really think it was Jamil?"

"Who else could it have been?" McKinley checked the number she'd dialed to confirm it. "The proof is right here." She showed Kristen her phone. "I dialed the right number, so it had to have been him."

"How old did the lil boy sound?"

"At least about five." McKinley shrugged her shoulders dismissively.

"Girl, this is too much for me. This is the type of shit you read about in one of them Keisha Ervin novels." Kristen waved her hand and got up. "I need a drink. You mind if I open up a bottle of wine?"

"No." McKinley walked over to the couch and sat down in a haze.

Seconds later, Kristen came back with a bottle of wine and two glasses. "Here." Kristen handed McKinley a glass of Pinot. "This will make you feel better."

McKinley took a long sip then looked at Kristen, and said, "What if this nigga got a baby?"

"Don't even claim that. It could've been his nephew, cousin, anybody," Kristen reasoned, praying to God she was right.

McKinley sat with the glass of wine in her hand, gazing blankly at the floor. It was time for her to leave Jamil alone. Holding onto him wasn't healthy. Child or no child, he'd told one too many lies and let her down too many times for her to continue to give him chance after chance. It was time for her to accept that this was who he was. She just couldn't figure out what the tears and long heartfelt conversations that lasted until the wee hours of the morning were for. None of it made sense.

Why did he profusely profess his love for her only to break her heart over and over again? Was it all a game that she didn't know she was participating in? The only thing she knew for sure was that she was tired of playing the guessing game. It was time for McKinley to put an end to the madness, even if it meant her heart breaking in the process. After finishing a whole bottle of Pinot, and hours of discussing the situation with Kristen, both women became tired.

Kristen yawned. "I am exhausted."

McKinley exhaled. "Me, too." Even after all of the talking they'd done, her stomach was still in knots.

"You want me to spend the night?" Kristen asked, stretching.

"Nah, I'll be okay." McKinley fiddled with her fingers.

"You sure? 'Cause I will stay if you want me to."

"I'm good." McKinley stood up and stretched her legs. "Go to your apartment and get some rest. I've taken up enough of your time as it is." She forced herself to smile.

"Girl, please, I ain't have shit else to do. Besides, you're my girl and you would've done the same thing for me. Hell, you *have* done the same thing for me." Kristen laughed.

"You silly." McKinley laughed, too.

"Well, look, call me if you need me." Kristen gave McKinley a warm hug.

"I will, and thanks again." McKinley hugged her back, then opened the door.

"No problem. Now go to sleep. Don't call him no more. You're only going to make yourself feel worse."

"I won't." McKinley assured, closing and locking the door behind her.

Alone, she placed her back against the door and took in the silence. The sound was excruciating. McKinley hated that she was going through this shit. It wasn't fair. She'd loved Jamil with every fiber of her being. She'd given him her all. She'd stood by his side during the good and the bad. When he fucked up, she was the one to pick up the pieces.

When he was afraid, she calmed his fears, but when she needed him, he was always unavailable. The whole situation was fucked up. Every time she thought they were making progress he always took ten steps backward, crushing her heart in two. It fucked her up that he wasn't emotionally responsible with her heart.

Time and time again Jamil would fill her heart with words of hope that he'd change and be a better man, and each time his actions proved differently. McKinley didn't know whether to believe his intentions or the outcome of his actions. It was all mind-numbing—loving someone who held her heart on a string like a marionette.

McKinley needed answers and fast. She needed to know what was going on with him and why he was being so insensitive of her feelings. It was obvious he was alive and well because she hadn't heard differently. Jamil was simply ignoring her, and the sad part was he didn't even have a reason to.

He was just selfish and until he decided to give up an explanation that was just how it was. Tired of debating with herself, McKinley wearily walked over to the stairs. She didn't know if she'd be able to sleep or not, but she had to lie down. McKinley didn't even make it up the steps before she heard the distinct sound of the front door opening.

Quickly, she spun around. Her heart was beating out of her chest in anticipation of seeing his face. Then he walked through the door. She could smell the enthralling scent of his Dolce & Gabbana cologne all the way from across the room. He looked better than he had the last time she saw him, crushing her spirit even more.

Jamil looked absolutely divine in a yellow BLVCK SCVLE T-shirt, Altamont fitted jeans and a brand new pair of $700 Dior Homme sneakers. McKinley was relieved to see that he was well, but confirmation of that signified her worst fear that he'd been dodging her on purpose.

She stormed down the steps. "Where in the hell have you been?"

"Calm down."

She pointed her index finger like a gun at his forehead. "Fuck that! Ain't no calming down! Why the fuck haven't you been answering your phone? I've been callin' you for days. I thought you were dead. But no, you're alive and well. So you've been sending me to voicemail all this time like I ain't shit?" She got up in his face. "Like I'm not yo' fiancée or should I give the ring back?" McKinley pulled off her ring and threw at him. "'Cause apparently the ring don't mean a damn thing."

"Will you let me explain?" Jamil tried reaching out for her, but McKinley snatched her hand away and shot him a look that could kill.

"Don't touch me. Touch whoever you done been wit' the last couple of days. Wit' yo' lousy ass! And who the fuck is Jamil?"

"What?" Jamil eyed her, confused.

"Nigga, don't act stupid. I called your phone and some boy named Jamil picked up the phone." McKinley rolled her neck. "Don't lie to me. Tell the truth. You gotta kid?"

"Man, I ain't come over here to talk about no kid." Jamil shook his head, never once giving her eye contact.

"What you mean you don't wanna talk about no kid? I dialed the right number, Jamil, and I swear I heard you talkin' in the background." McKinley's voice cracked.

"You know what? I don't even know why the fuck I bother." Jamil's nostrils flared. "This why I can't never talk to you 'cause you always on some other shit. You always assuming the worst. I know, I'm wrong. I don't ever do shit right. What's new? Shit, fuck this, I'm up." He turned to leave.

McKinley knew she should've called his bluff and let him walk out the door, but the part of her heart that needed him more than she needed air to breathe wouldn't allow it.

"Jamil, wait." She jumped in front of him and blocked his path.

"Nah." He shook his head. "I'm tired of this shit. I came over here to talk to you. Not be accused of a bunch of foul shit."

McKinley gazed into his eyes. A world of pain hid behind his irises. She wondered how long it had been lying there. She'd never seen Jamil look so sad before. She felt like shit. Maybe she had overreacted? Maybe the boy who answered his phone had been his cousin?

"Will you calm down? I just don't understand what's going on."

"Okay, but instead of jumpin' to conclusions, how about you listen to me sometimes?"

"I'm sorry." McKinley shrugged her shoulders and shook

her head.

"I'm for real, McKinley. Don't come to me on no shit like this again. You gotta learn how to trust me. I got enough on my plate as it is." Jamil turned his face and looked away, mad.

McKinley stuck her face in front of his. "I understand. I was just worried about you."

"I don't even wanna talk about that no more. Just come lay down wit' me. I'm tired and I wanna lie down," he said, going up the stairs.

McKinley followed Jamil to her bedroom. Once there, she climbed into bed while he took off his sneakers. Once his shoes were off, Jamil got into bed and lay behind her. His strong arms enveloped her waist. Jamil placed a soft kiss on the nape of her neck.

"I love you," he whispered.

"I love you too," McKinley said reluctantly.

Sure, this was the side of Jamil she loved; it was just sad he couldn't be this way all the time. McKinley just couldn't allow herself to fall back into the same routine just 'cause the touch of his hand on her skin made her feel alive. This shit had to stop. She was tired of feeling like she was the only one dying. No way could he disappear for four days and this be it.

"Uh ah." She shot up.

There was no way she could just lay down and pretend that the last four days hadn't happened.

"I can't do this."

"Do what?" Jamil mumbled.

"I can't do *this* anymore." McKinley stressed the word this.

"What's wrong wit' you now, McKinley?" Jamil huffed, opening his eyes.

"I'll tell you exactly what's wrong with me. I'm tired of you doing whatever the fuck you wanna do, then when I step to you about it you flip out on me and make it seem like *I'm* crazy. I know what happened. It's not okay that you do this kind of stuff and I just sit here and fuckin' take it."

"C'mon, babe. I'm tired, just lay down. We'll talk about this in the morning." Jamil tried to get her to lie back down.

"No, I don't wanna lay down, and we gon' talk about this right now," she hissed, pushing him away.

"I want you to explain to me how you can propose to me and disappear on me all in the same damn day. What kind of shit is that, and who does shit like that? You claim to love me so much, but every chance you get you're hurtin' me. And I don't understand why you do me like this." McKinley began to cry. "Oh, I know why. You do it 'cause you can."

"Stop." Jamil sat up and tried to hold her, but McKinley wasn't willing to let her defenses down.

"No! If we're gonna get married, I need for you to change. I'm tired of yo' mouth making promises, but your actions showing me something different. I'm tired of one minute we're good and then within a blink of an eye it's some bullshit all over again. This shit is driving me insane."

"I told you I was gonna change. But change takes time, McKinley. You gotta give me a chance to do it," Jamil reasoned.

"I've given you three years to change. If it ain't happened by now then it ain't gon' happen," McKinley shrieked.

"So what you sayin'?"

McKinley sat quietly and collected herself. "I think we need to take a break," she finally said.

"A break?" Jamil looked at her sideways. "What the fuck you mean, 'a break'? We ain't takin' no fuckin' break. If we ain't gon' be together, we ain't gon' be together. Ain't no in-between."

"Then I guess we ain't gon' be together then," McKinley replied calmly.

"Word? So that's it?" Jamil stared at her surprised.

"Yeah."

"A'ight." Jamil got out of the bed and put on his shoes.

McKinley willed herself to breathe. With each second that passed, it seemed like she was going to faint. Her stomach was in knots as she watched Jamil grab his keys. If she wanted him now was the time to stop him, but the further he got down the hall the firmer she stood on her decision. This would be good for the both of them. McKinley just prayed that her walking away wouldn't be the biggest mistake of her life.

"The problem is that you know where my heart stands. You use it against me."

Dawn Richards

"Broken Record"

When she'd made it up in her mind that leaving Jamil alone was the right move to make, McKinley never considered the fact that being without him would cause more than a broken heart. Being without Jamil made her feel like she'd died one-hundred times. Every day was like *Groundhog's Day*. Every morning she relived the fact that he was gone and never coming back. She would never hear the sound of his footsteps coming up the stairs.

She wouldn't feel him lying next to her in the middle of the night. She wouldn't get to smell the sweet scent of his skin. The sound of his laughter wouldn't fill the house up anymore. Every moment of the day she spent alone. When the phone rang, everything in her hoped that it would be him on the other end, begging for her forgiveness. She'd called him and left him messages, begging him to call her, but Jamil hadn't called once.

It had been two weeks since she heard his voice or saw his face. It was like he'd fallen off the face of the earth. Curled up in bed, McKinley gazed at the wall. Tears slid out of the corners of her eyes at a rapid speed. She'd hardly eaten in days. When she closed her eyes at night, the only thing she dreamed of was him. No matter what she did, thoughts of Jamil haunted her brain.

Her friends said that in time the pain would get better, but McKinley didn't believe it. To be without Jamil was worse than being with him. The inconsistencies of their relationship she could handle, but the constant pang in her heart was torture. She wanted her baby back. Everyone around her would call her dumb, but she didn't care. They weren't the ones suffering.

McKinley didn't know what to do. Begging him to take her back made her feel like a complete and utter fool, but every second she breathed air knowing he wasn't hers anymore killed her. Fuck pride, McKinley had to get her man back. Using her cell phone, she called him. Each ring felt like death. It hurt her even more when he didn't pick up.

McKinley hung up the phone and burst into tears. *How can he just ignore me like this,* she wondered when her phone rang. McKinley looked at the screen. It was Jamil. A sense of relief flooded over her body.

"Hello?" Her voice quivered.

"What's up? You called?" he asked nonchalantly.

McKinley could hear music and people talking in the background. It sounded as if he was at a club or a bar.

"Yeah, you know I did," she answered with a slight attitude.

"Look, I ain't call you to argue."

"I didn't call you to argue either," McKinley explained.

"Well, what's up then?" Jamil asked dryly.

"Will you please come home? I'm sorry. I made a mistake. I thought that breaking up wit' you was the best thing to do, but it wasn't. I miss you," she cried. "And I just want you to come home."

"I don't know if I can do that," Jamil said regrettably.

"Why?" McKinley said, taken aback by his answer.

"'Cause, man. You were right. We needed to fall back from each other. And I mean, I miss you and everything, but I don't think we ready to just jump back into being wit' each other."

"That's a bunch of bullshit and you know it," McKinley cried out. "I love you and you love me."

"I never said that I didn't love you. Love just don't go away overnight," Jamil confessed.

"So that's it? You just don't wanna be wit' me no more?" McKinley stopped crying.

"I ain't tryin' to be rude or nothin', but can I call you back?"

McKinley held the phone stunned.

"Hello?" Jamil said.

"Yeah," she replied, feeling like if she let him get off the phone she'd never hear from him again.

"Can I call you right back?"

"Whatever, Jamil." McKinley rolled her eyes and hung up the phone.

"What the hell am I sittin' up here cryin' over this nigga for?" McKinley said out loud to herself, pissed off.

Fed up, she got out of the bed and turned on the light.

"The hell with this shit," she spat. "I'm sittin' over her feeling like I'm dying and this nigga couldn't care less, he out partying. Fuck this."

McKinley went into the master bathroom and looked at herself in the mirror. She looked a mess. She hadn't combed her hair in days. Her face looked pale and dry. Dried-up tear stains scarred her cheeks. Tired of looking and feeling disgusting, she turned on the shower and got in. The hot water running over her body made her feel as if she was being hugged.

Once her body was clean and fresh, she turned off the water and got out. After drying off, McKinley brushed her teeth and washed her face, then grabbed her Wild Cherry Blossom lotion and walked back into her room. Annoyed with the silence that enveloped her, she popped a mix CD into her Blu Ray player. The first song that began to play was Jazmine Sullivan's fuck-him-girl anthem "Holding You Down." McKinley sat on the edge of her bed and began lathering on lotion while singing along.

It's a shame that you don't care enough,
To even give me half the love,
I give to you,
I live for you baby,
I'm ashamed to say that I'm to blame for how you act,
'Cause I keep comin' back.

McKinley couldn't sing a lick, but every lyric from the song resonated deep within her soul. After every inch of her skin was covered with lotion, McKinley went over to her walk-in closet and pulled out the most uncomplicated outfit she could find. Then Barbra Streisand's "Don't Rain on My Parade," from the iconic movie, *Funny Girl,* came on.

Don't tell me not to live,

Just sit and putter,

Life's candy and the sun's a ball of butter.

She stood up and danced like a Broadway dancer.

Fuck staying in the house sulking. It was time for her to live. She wasn't going to let Jamil rain on her parade. He was living and going on with his life, so why shouldn't she make the same moves? Dressed in a Camilla and Marc, print Georgette dress with a scoop neck, cutout shoulders and short flutter sleeves, McKinley placed on a cute pair of gold sandals.

Standing in front of the mirror, she pulled her hair up into a sleek ponytail, dabbed on a little pink lip gloss, grabbed her house keys and headed out the door. But to McKinley's surprise, as soon as she stepped out of the door, Jamil got off the elevator. McKinley stood frozen, wondering could he hear the loud thumping in her chest that sounded like a drum beat.

"Where you going?" he asked, eying her up and down.

"Why?" McKinley replied. She didn't want to tell him the truth, which was she had no idea where she was going.

"'Cause I want you to take a walk with me," Jamil said.

McKinley looked away, hating that Jamil's presence had

such an impact on her. Every time she came near him, her entire being was reduced to a mere puddle. Her mouth begged her to tell him to kick rocks, but the pull he had on her heartstrings triumphed and she found herself saying, "Okay."

In a daze, McKinley boarded the elevator with Jamil in silence. She was all prepared to say fuck him and to start moving on with her life. But just like every other time she was ready to take that step into the unknown, Jamil appeared, causing her to steer off course. Outside the cool night air kissed their skin as they walked side by side down the street.

"So what do you wanna talk to me about?" McKinley said at once.

"I wanted to tell you that I'm sorry. I know that I haven't treated you right, but I'm tryin', McKinley. I love you and I don't wanna lose you."

"I can't tell. I haven't heard from you in two weeks," McKinley said simply.

"And by no means do I want you to think that was easy for me. I'm fucked up by this, too. I haven't been able to sleep at night," he confessed.

"Well, how come when I called you, you didn't answer the phone?" she countered.

"I mean, what was I gon' say? What I did was fucked up and nothin' I said was gon' make you feel any better, so I just decided to fall back for a minute."

McKinley took in his words and let them digest in her brain. She desperately wanted to believe what he was telling her, but she'd heard this same speech one too many times before to trust in his word.

"So what now?" she asked, walking at a slow pace.

"If you allow me the chance, I wanna show you that I can be everything you need me to be and more," Jamil said after a pause.

McKinley closed her eyes and inhaled deeply. She'd prayed to God repeatedly to stop the nagging pain that lay in the center of her chest. Now was her chance to end it. This was it, after this, Jamil would get no more chances. If he didn't get it right this time then she was done for good.

"I'll give you another chance, but if you don't do right by me this time, I'm done," she said with a sudden fierceness.

"I swear to *God*, this time it's gon' be different," Jamil assured, smoothing back her hair.

McKinley relished his touch and said a silent prayer to God that this time the desires of her heart would come to fruition.

XoXo

It was the middle of summer and McKinley was on cloud nine. She and Jamil had been getting along tremendously. They hadn't fought one time. Jamil had been on his best behavior.

He'd become more attentive. He catered to her every whim.

Whatever free time he had to spare when he wasn't working was spent with her. He'd even been assisting with the wedding plans.

Two hundred and fifty of their closest family and friends would attend their nuptials. Their wedding date had been set for September 8th. McKinley couldn't wait to become Mrs. Jamil Thompson. Her first duty as his wife would be to give him the son that he'd always wanted. That day after meeting with their wedding planner and going over table settings and centerpieces, McKinley hopped into her Mercedes G Wagon and headed back home to meet up with Jamil.

They were going to go over the seating chart. It had been hell trying to figure out where to seat everyone. As McKinley pulled up to her building, her cell phone began to ring. It was Jamil. A huge smile spread across her face.

"Hey, baby," she said, parking her car.

"Where you at?" he asked.

"Just pulling up to the house, why? Where are you?" she asked, turning off the engine.

"Please don't be mad, but I'm runnin' a lil bit behind."

"How behind, Jamil?" McKinley groaned.

"Like an hour."

"Are you kidding me? I just rushed home, thinkin' I was gon' meet you here."

"My bad. I'ma be there as soon as I can," he promised.

"Okay, Jamil, hurry up," McKinley insisted.

"I am."

"Alright, love you," she uttered.

"Love you, too."

Since Jamil would be arriving late, McKinley decided to take matters into her own hands and start doing the seating charts on her own. She had no time to waste. Every second of the day counted. Plus, she had a million other things that needed to be completed as well. She couldn't put the seating charts off another day.

Once the elevator doors opened, McKinley stormed into her apartment on a mission. Dropping her bags at the door, she quickly began creating the perfect seating chart. Almost two hours later she'd only gotten two of the tables done and was past frustrated. Annoyed that Jamil hadn't showed up yet, she texted him.

To: Jamil
Where are you?
Sent:
Fri, Aug 12, 4:50 pm

To: McKinley
I'ma b there in a min.
Received:
Mon, Aug 12, 4:52 pm

To: Jamil
What's a min, Jamil?
Sent:
Mon, Aug 12, 4:54 pm

To: McKinley
Half an hour
Received:
Mon, Aug 12, 5:01 pm

Overwhelmed, McKinley threw down her phone and went over to the refrigerator. Her stomach was growling so loud it sounded like she'd passed gas. Needing something quick and fresh to eat, she fixed herself a ham sandwich with celery sticks and peanut butter on the side. Trying her best not to focus on the time, McKinley sat at the dining room table and ate her food while watching *Dancing with the Stars*. Before she knew it, she'd finished eating, the program had gone off and Jamil still hadn't shown up. Fed up, she dialed his number.

"What's up?" Jamil said in a low tone.

"I cannot believe you starting this shit again. I've been sittin' here, waitin' on you all afternoon. Where the fuck are you?" McKinley yelled.

"Yo, I can't be talkin' to you right now."

"What you say?" McKinley replied, taken aback.

"Let me call you back. I'm in the middle of something."

"Jamil, I swear to God if you hang up this phone I'm officially done fuckin' wit' you," McKinley warned.

"Babe, just give me a minute," he pleaded.

But before McKinley could reply the sound of gun fire caused her heart to leap out of her chest and fall flat onto the floor.

"Jamil." She called out for him, but got no reply. "Jamil," she screamed, praying to God he'd answer. "Jamil!"

Part Two

"And the anger and the sorrow mixed up leaves the mistrust. Now it gets tough to ever love again."

Jay Z

"Allure"

McKinley had worn the same clothes for two days. She sat Indian style in the center of her king-sized bed, clutching Jamil's pillow, wishing that he was there. It was the middle of the night, but so what? Sleep had become an insufferable pastime she could do without. A pain so strong resonated from her ribs and her eyes, causing an abundance of tears to stream down her face. He was gone and with each second that passed by that conclusion became clearer. She wished this time was like the other times they'd fought and he'd left.

She'd cry until her throat was sore, he'd come back, rock her pussy to sleep, then promise that everything would be okay. But two days ago, everything changed. He was brutally gunned down outside of his apartment and she was forced to deal with the fact that this time he was gone for good. She would never feel his lips on hers or have the pleasure of being wrapped in his warm embrace. All of her days from now on would be long, drawn out and insignificant. She'd forever be chasing pavements, instead of obsessing over him.

"It's not fair," she sobbed, hitting his pillow with her fist.

It wasn't fair that they never got to say good-bye with words. It wasn't fair that he was killed for reasons unknown. And it most certainly wasn't fair that she sat alone, gazing at a picture of him, wondering why he couldn't be a part of her future. Doubled over in pain, McKinley cried tears of sorrow and loneliness. The five-carat canary-yellow diamond ring, closet full of designer shoes and dresses and Hermes Birkin bags wouldn't comfort her in her time of need.

McKinley would give it all, her heart, her home, her clothes, anything she owned just to have him back. Reluctantly, she let go of the pillow and placed her face into her hands. An eerie quietness surrounded her. Just as she was about to release a blood-curdling scream to the heavens up above, a thunderous bang came crashing through her front door. Scared out of her mind, she sat frozen stiff. From her bedroom, she could hear the sound of heavy footsteps run rampant throughout her apartment.

Suddenly, the door to her bedroom swung open. Five men dressed in black charged inside with flashlights pointing her way. McKinley turned her face and lifted her arm to shield her eyes from the blaring lights.

"Freeze! Put your hands behind your head and stand against the wall," the federal agent ordered.

"What the hell are you all doing in my house?" McKinley demanded to know, ignoring their orders.

"Ma'am, I'm only going to ask you one more time. Please get off of the bed."

"Not until you tell me what the fuck—"

Before McKinley knew it, her bedroom light was on and her petite body was being dragged from the bed and placed up against the wall. McKinley let out a scream for help so loud she swore her neighbors would hear.

"Shut up!" the man ordered.

"What the hell is going on?" she demanded to know.

"We have a warrant to search your place—"

"Sir, we found a safe," one of the agents said, pulling a silver safe out of the floor.

"And we're bringing you in for questioning," the federal agent explained.

"But I didn't do anything. What is going on?" she wailed.

McKinley was so incoherent that she didn't even realize she'd been spun around. Everything was moving so fast, she felt high. The federal agents walked past her in slow motion as if she wasn't even there. McKinley stood back and watched helplessly with tears in her eyes as they ransacked her place. The Matteograssi bed that she and Jamil slept in, made love in, shared dreams in was broken down.

The Ligne Roset side table he used to place his cell phone on at night was turned over as if it wasn't worth anything. The federal agents searched relentlessly for some kind of evidence she didn't know existed. The very pillow she held close to her heart a second ago was ripped down the middle, exposing a wealth of white feathers. Some of Jamil's jewelry and clothes that he kept there were thrown on the floor.

"The safe is filled with money," one of the agents informed his captain.

"What is going on? What are you looking for?"

"Okay, men, we've found what we need. Let's wrap this up. Agent Franklin, take this young lady down to the car. She's coming with us."

XoXo

"Thanks for coming to get me." McKinley massaged her wrists, coming out of the federal building.

Kristen wrapped her arm around McKinley's shoulder. "Are you okay?"

McKinley threw up her arms. "No, look at me."

Kristen hated to admit it, but McKinley looked horrible. Dried tears stained her caramel face. Her hair was all over her head. The Jill Stuart silk chiffon print maxi dress with a ruffle overlay at the bodice and cascading ruffles at the skirt that she'd worn two days before was a worn and tattered mess. Kristen could even smell a foul stench come from her body.

"Kristen, I don't know what I'm going to do," McKinley explained, getting into the car.

"I ain't tryin' to be funny, but do you mind if we let the window down?" Kristen held her nose.

"Fuck you, bitch. I know I stink."

"Hey, I'm just sayin'. I need to have a clear mind while I drive." Kristen laughed.

"All jokes aside," McKinley said seriously. "Shit is fucked

up. They've seized all of our accounts. I don't have a dime to my name."

"For real?"

"You think I'm playin'?"

"Damn," Kristen said as she drove back to their apartment.

"I can't believe this shit is happening to me." McKinley stared out the window wearily.

"Everything's gonna be alright, McKinley. I got a little stash of money put up. It's not much, but I'll help you the best that I can." Kristen pulled into her personal parking space.

"No, Kristen. I can't take money from you."

"Girl, please. You're my best friend. I ain't gon' let you go without."

"Thank you." McKinley gave her a slight smile.

After saying hello to the doorman, McKinley and Kristen boarded the elevator in silence. Once at her door, McKinley inhaled deeply and prepared herself for the worst. Gradually, she pushed open the door. Her living room was a wreck. The curtains were pulled. Mirrors were broken. Cushions from the couch were slit open and thrown about. The coffee table was turned over. Papers were sprawled all over the floor. McKinley could only imagine what the rest of the place looked like.

"Muthafuckin' cocksuckers," she yelled, pissed.

"I can't believe they did this." Kristen gazed around, amazed by the carnage.

"This is some bullshit," McKinley exclaimed, running from room to room.

Carefully, Kristen picked up a black-and-white photo of McKinley that was on the floor. Jamil had taken it while they were on vacation in St. Bart's two summers ago. In the photo McKinley smiled gleefully. Rays from the sun shined down onto her honey-colored skin. McKinley looked strikingly beautiful in the picture.

"They straight fucked up all of my shit. What the fuck am I going to do?" McKinley reentered the living area.

"Okay, I know it's a lot, but just calm down." Kristen placed the picture on top of the mantle. "So what now?" Kristen asked.

"Shit, I don't know. You tell me. I'm a broke, twenty-five-year-old woman with hardly any work experience and not a pot to piss in. My fiancé is dead. I mean, how could my life get any worse?"

The words hadn't even settled into the atmosphere before there was a loud knock on McKinley's door.

"You expecting company?" Kristen turned and looked at her.

"No. It's probably one of the neighbors. They've been bringing food and flowers all week," McKinley said, slowly easing up from the floor. "Who is it?"

"Leah."

McKinley gazed over her shoulder at Kristen with a perplexed expression on her face. She didn't know anyone named Leah. Slowly, she unlocked the door and found a well-dressed woman who looked to be in her mid-thirties, standing there.

"May I help you?" McKinley asked politely with her hand on the knob.

"McKinley, right?" Leah asked, clutching her Carlos Falchi clutch purse.

"And you are?" McKinley ignored her question, afraid she might be a detective.

"Leah Thompson…Jamil's wife."

The only thing McKinley could do was chuckle. *This chick is clearly delusional,* she thought. *There is no way on God's green earth that my Jamil was married, especially not to this chick. Hell, I have been with him for three years, so where in the hell has this chick been the whole time? 'Cause he was here with me at least four to five days out of the week. Yeah, this bitch is crazy, so let me shut this chick down like a bad Ferris wheel, so I can get back to being depressed.*

"Look, lady, I don't know who you are, but—"

"As I stated before, I'm his wife," Leah said with an even tone. "So to make this as simple as possible, let me get you up to speed. Jamil and I have been married for nine years and we have two lovely children, Brianna and Jamil Jr."

McKinley immediately remembered the phone call where

the lil' boy answered the phone. *So that was his son,* she thought.

"We have a home, or shall I say, a mansion on Star Island, and an apartment in Tribeca, New York, and a beach house in Malibu. I've known about you for about two years now."

"So why are you just sayin' something now?" McKinley snapped.

"'Cause you weren't the first woman he stepped out on me with and you for damn sure weren't the last. To be exact, it's me, then his other girlfriend slash baby mama, Tanay, then you. And yes, to be clear, he was seeing all three of us at the same time. Did it hurt in the beginning? Yes. Do I care now? No. 'Cause I knew this day would come where I would get everything."

McKinley stood speechless. She hadn't even blinked she was so stunned.

"Yeah, I know it's a shock. It was also a shock to me when I found out that he'd proposed to you with a five-carat diamond ring a couple of months ago and you tearfully said yes," Leah said mockingly. "Oh, but wait, there's more. Because of my husband's untimely passing, I now have to tie up all of his loose ends. See, this fairly modest apartment that you've been living in is under Jamil's name and since I'm his beneficiary I now have control of it. So I've decided to sell this apartment immediately, which gives you thirty days to vacate the premises."

"What? You've got to be kidding, right?" McKinley said in disbelief.

"No, honey, sorry, I'm not. Well, look, now that we've gotten a chance to chat I have to be off. I do have a funeral to plan." Leah secured her purse underneath her arm. "It was nice meeting you, McKinley. I wish you the best of luck. Smooches." Leah blew McKinley a kiss then sashayed off down the hallway.

"What was that all about?" Kristen asked standing up.

"Oh, just the usual, you know," McKinley scoffed. "That was Jamil's wife. She came by to tell me that I have thirty days to vacate the premises. So I guess I was wrong. My life *can* get worse."

"O…M…G, really?" Kristen said, aghast.

"Yes. This whole time that muthafucka was living a double life. Here I am thinking I'm the only one and he got a whole wife, two kids *and* a baby mama. I was with him for three years and all I have to show for it is a bunch of clothes and a whack-ass engagement ring. This bitch gets everything and I'm left with nothing. I gave up my family and my friends for him. He had me thinkin' we were gon' be together forever." McKinley cried hysterically.

"So what are you going to do?"

McKinley stood, trembling with fear. There was only one way out of her predicament. The one thing she'd been dreading the most. The word alone made her cringe and brought on bouts of anxiety.

"I guess I'll have to," she swallowed hard, "go home."

"I guess I met you for a reason. Only time can tell."

J Cole feat Drake
"In The Morning"

After two weeks of packing up her things and having them shipped to St. Louis, courtesy of her mother, it was time for McKinley to bid farewell. It was her last day in Miami before flying home to St. Louis. She'd truly missed Miami. She didn't know how she'd live without the smell of sea salt or seeing the leaves from the palm trees sway in the wind. She'd yearn for the scrumptious food, colorful printed clothes, all-night club scene and great weather. More than anything she'd miss all of the time she and Jamil spent there.

When they'd met three years prior, while she was on vacation, he'd swept her off her feet and she'd never left. Now she was being forced to leave. Parts of her hated him for the lies he'd told and for making her feel like she was the only one. But for the last three years of her life all she'd known was the love he'd shown her.

After strolling the beach one last time, McKinley placed her orange, suede, peep-toe heels back on and headed to Hotel Victor for an early dinner. As she walked, the sun was just starting to set when suddenly she spotted him. There he was, sitting on the edge of his silver, SL 65 AMG, with his left hand in his pocket, surrounded by his homeboys. Everything about him screamed heartbreaker and to keep it moving, but McKinley couldn't take her eyes off of him.

He was six feet, one hundred ninety pounds with skin the color of peanut butter. A blue Yankee's cap cocked to the left covered his low cut, but enhanced his Asian-inspired eyes, chiseled cheekbones and soft kissable lips. She didn't know if he had a girl, but visions of what they could be filled her mind. He was the type of nigga she wanted to wake up in the morning and cook breakfast for, forget her past for, shed tears for; but McKinley had bigger fish to fry. Like figuring out where she'd get her next buck from. Using the common sense God gave her, she made her way into the hotel's lobby instead of giving into temptation.

Hotel Victor was one of South Beach's premier hotels. Their luxury suites, breathtaking views and spa treatments were one of a kind. McKinley especially loved their use of vibrant colors and modern furniture. Vix wasn't just another South Beach restaurant, it was an experience. It provided artistry in every aspect of the restaurant, from the cuisine to their elegant paintings. The tables were made of beautiful marble slabs. Each one was stylishly decorated with vanilla tea candles and twenty-four karat flatware. There were a mixture of crème and mustard colored chairs, trimmed in brown. McKinley was seated at a table for two by the window, which was open.

A soothing breeze kissed her skin as she skimmed through the menu. Once her order was placed, McKinley pulled out her cell to call her mother, but the sight of Jamil's face on her screen brought her to tears. Overwhelmed with emotions, she threw the phone back inside her purse as well as her ring. She couldn't imagine what her life would be like now that Jamil was dead.

Not only was he her boyfriend, but her mentor and friend; so when the proposal of marriage came up, there was no way she could say no. But now, McKinley was on her own, with little to no money and forced to move back in with her mother. Unknowingly, a tear slipped from her eye and she began to cry. Choking back the tears that filled her throat, McKinley got up and walked quickly to the restroom to gather her emotions.

Once her emotions were in check, she placed on a new coat of Chanel lip gloss and exited the restroom. On her way back to her table, she locked eyes with the caramel thug from outside. Pleased to see her again, he strolled toward her with a smile. McKinley hoped and prayed that he couldn't tell she'd been crying as he approached.

"How you doing?" He gently took her hand, fascinated by her facial features.

"Fine, and you?" McKinley smiled.

"Better now."

"Really?" She laughed.

"Yeah. So what's your name?"

"McKinley."

"Nice to meet you McKinley." He looked at her in awe.

"Nice to meet you, too…"

"Koran." He shook his head. "My bad. It's just that you look like someone I used to know." Koran referred to his late wife, Whitney, who had lost her battle with cancer six years before.

If it wasn't for the height and weight difference, McKinley would've been a dead ringer for Whitney.

"I get that a lot." McKinley chuckled.

"So umm... are you here with somebody?" Koran looked around. "I don't wanna get you in trouble or nothin'," he joked.

"You good, no actually, I'm here by myself." McKinley stared him directly in the eye while still holding onto his hand.

"That's what's up." Koran nodded. "So uh... you gon' let my hand go or what?"

"Oh, I'm sorry." McKinley drew her hand back and blushed.

"It's all good. I was just fuckin' wit' you. Were you on your way out, or have you already been seated?"

"I've already been seated. I was just on my way back to my table."

"You need someone to go wit' you," Koran flirted.

"If you want to."

"So, McKinley, what's a pretty girl like you doing walkin' down the streets of Miami by yourself this time of the day? It's a lot of bad guys out here. You gotta be safe."

"Are you one of the bad guys or are you a bad guy tryin'

Keisha Ervin

to be good?"

"I guess you could say I'm a little bit of both. Hopefully you'll stick around long enough to find out."

"Maybe I will."

Koran normally wasn't the type of dude to go after a female so hard, but he had to get to know the woman who resembled his late wife. Besides that, there was something about McKinley that told him she needed a real man in her life. She'd caught his attention as soon as she turned the corner. At that moment he knew he had to holla at her. She was stunningly beautiful, but in her own unique way. Due to the warm Miami heat, she wore a ribbed cashmere polo shirt and a pair of silk twill Louis Vuitton shorts. A topaz and gold braid necklace with black diamonds designed by Janis Savitt completed her look. Girlfriend was fly, and from the way she talked, it seemed like she had her mind right.

"So, Koran, do you live here?" McKinley quizzed.

"Nah, I just came here for a wedding."

"Excuse me, sir, would you like something to drink?" a server asked.

"Yeah, I'll have whatever she's having," Koran replied.

"You might not want to do that." McKinley snickered.

"Why not?" Koran eyed her perplexed.

"I'm having a shot of Patron."

"Man, please, you made it seem like you was talkin' about

– 102 –

something." He waved her off. "I'll have two shots of Patron," he said to the waiter.

"Bring me out another as well," McKinley said to the server too.

"So this how we doing it?" Koran grinned.

"Might as well," McKinley shrugged her shoulders.

Seconds later, their waiter returned with their drinks and placed them on the table before them.

"Okay, here we go." McKinley held up her shot glass.

"Cheers!" Koran tapped his glass against hers then quickly guzzled it down.

McKinley did the same.

"Whew," she grimaced, shaking her head.

"You think you can handle another?" Koran smiled mischievously.

"I can handle anything you can dish out."

XoXo

The following morning McKinley awoke in a drunken haze. Lying on her back, she gazed up at the ceiling, which seemed to be moving from side to side. Feeling nauseated, she quickly snapped her eyes shut again. *Where am I,* she thought. The seven tequila shots from the night before had completely clouded her memory. The only thing she knew for sure was that she felt disgusting. There was crust in the corners of her eyes and her tongue and lips were dry.

She couldn't wait to get to a toothbrush and a wash cloth. Figuring it was best she got up and pieced the last ten hours of her life together, McKinley reopened her eyes and pulled back the covers. To her shock and dismay, she found that she was stark naked.

"What the hell?" she uttered, pulling the covers back over her.

Then out of nowhere she heard the sound of a loud snort and realized that she wasn't alone. Scrunching her forehead, McKinley gradually turned her head to the right and found a toned muscular back facing her. *Umm*, she thought as a still-sleeping Koran turned over and faced her. *Oh, my God, I slept with the guy from the restaurant.*

"Oh, my God," she groaned, running her hands down her face. "What were you thinking, McKinley?" she whispered.

Out of nowhere, as if an alarm was set off inside of her, McKinley remembered her flight.

"Shit," she shrieked, jumping out of the bed.

Yes, she was mortified by her drunken rendezvous with the stranger, but she'd deal with that later. There was no way on God's green earth that she was missing her flight. She couldn't; after that day she had no place to stay. Quietly, McKinley searched the hotel room for her things. She and Koran's clothes and shoes were thrown about all over the room.

Locating her bra, which was by the door, she bent over to pick it up, but a wave of dizziness swarmed her head. *I will never drink tequila again,* she swore, standing up straight. With as much speed as she could muster, McKinley whizzed around the room, gathering and putting on her things. Minutes later, she was fully dressed and ready to go. With her hand on the knob, she glanced over her shoulder at Koran who was still asleep.

She wondered if she should at least say good-bye. But what kind of good-bye would it be? *Hey, it was nice having sex with you. I'll see you later,* or *glad we fucked; too bad we'll never see each other again.* Deciding that saying good-bye wasn't the best idea, McKinley stared at him a second more. The sight of his handsome face, lying there looking so peaceful brought back memories of Jamil. She knew that it was dumb, being as though Jamil was a lying, cheating whore, but she couldn't help but feel like she was betraying him.

Hell, the man had just died a couple of weeks before. Besides, sleeping with Koran had just been another mistake to add to her list of fuck-ups in life. Remembering her flight, McKinley shrugged her shoulders and opened the door, vowing that from that moment forward she would do everything in her power to get her life back on track.

XoXo

McKinley said a silent prayer to God, thanking Him for allowing her to make it to the airport in just enough time to board the plane. It had been a race against the clock, but she made it. Sitting in her seat, she turned her cell phone off and placed it inside her purse. Closing her eyes, she leaned her head back and turned it to the side facing the window. The hangover she was nursing was kicking her ass. She couldn't wait for the plane to take off, so she could ask a flight attendant for some aspirins. What McKinley didn't know was that in a few seconds her headache was about to take a turn from bad to worse.

"Excuse me," Koran said, easing his way down the aisle.

He'd barely made it to the airport. If it wasn't for his daughter calling him to say good morning he'd probably still be asleep. He just knew that when he woke up McKinley would still be by his side, but to his surprise she was already gone. He wondered if it had all been a dream. Maybe he'd conjured the whole thing up in his head. All he knew for sure was that he had to get home to his baby girl.

Koran found his seat, which was in the very back of the plane. *Goddamnit, I got the aisle seat*, he thought. Koran hated the aisle seat. Flight attendants were always bumping into him and he couldn't see out the window good. Since he refused to check in luggage, Koran opened the overhead compartment and squeezed his bag inside. Dying to sit down and relax, he sat down next to the young lady who lucked up and got a window seat. As Koran adjusted himself in his seat his left elbow accidently nudged the woman.

"Sorry," he said as she turned and looked at him with disdain.

"You!" McKinley sat up surprised.

"Me?" Koran shot back.

"Yeah, you." McKinley rolled her neck. "What the hell are you doing here? Are you some kind of stalker or something?"

"Man, please, you wish." Koran waved her off. "I'm heading home to St. Louis."

"Okay, now this is too much. I'm heading home to St. Louis, too. You sure you're not no hired hit man?" McKinley looked around nervously.

Maybe whoever killed Jamil was planning on killing her next.

"If I was would I tell you?" Koran shot sarcastically.

"This is some bullshit," McKinley said, outraged.

"You can say that again," Koran agreed.

"Everyone, please fasten your seatbelts. Delta Airlines, flight sixty-eight, leaving Miami, Florida and heading to Atlanta, Georgia is preparing for takeoff. Please turn off all electronic devices."

"So, you're trying to tell me that none of this was planned?" McKinley said in a low tone while buckling her seat belt. "That you didn't seek me out on purpose and that you didn't book a seat on the same flight as me on purpose? This is just all purely coincidental?" She eyed him skeptically.

"Yes," Koran replied annoyed.

"I don't care nothin' about you having an attitude. I'm tryin' to make sure you're not out to kill me."

"The question is, why are you so concerned with somebody tryin' to kill you?" Koran stared at her.

McKinley sat speechless. There was no way she was gonna tell him about Jamil.

"That's beside the point," she huffed. "Did somebody hire you to kill me or what?" she shouted, causing everyone on the plane to turn around.

"Will you shut the fuck up?" Koran clasped his hand over her mouth. "Everything's fine, she's just rehearsing for a play she's in, sorry," he assured the other passengers.

Once everyone was settled back into their seats, Koran released his hand from McKinley's mouth.

"I hope your hands are clean." She screwed up her face.

"Fuck all of that. Let me tell you something." Koran pulled her close to him and whispered into her ear. "If I wanted you dead you'd be dead by now, so you can stop wit' all that rah-rah. Now sit yo' ass back and enjoy the fuckin' ride."

"Well, excuse me. You don't have to be rude," McKinley scoffed as the plane took off on the runway.

McKinley gripped the arms of the seat tight. She hated flying. The thought of being that high up in the air with no safety net was terrifying. McKinley squeezed her eyes tight and repeated to herself "Oh, God! Oh, God! Oh, God! Oh, God! Oh, God!"

Koran glanced over at her and noticed her chanting. Because she was holding on to the seat so tight, her knuckles were stark white. Koran wanted to be a dick and ignore her whining, but every time he gazed at her, thoughts of his late wife, Whitney, appeared. She hated to fly too.

"Are you gon' be doin' this the whole flight?" he asked.

"Doing what?" McKinley opened her right eye.

"Whining."

"I'm not whining. I'm praying. Something you obviously know nothin' about," she snapped.

Koran ignored her comment and said, "Whatever you doing, can you stop? It's gettin' on my nerves."

"Oh, my God, you are such a jerk. You've never met someone who's afraid of takeoff?" McKinley asked.

"At least they appreciated my help." He thought back to Whitney again.

"How are you helping me? By being an asshole?" McKinley quipped.

Koran ignored her sarcasm. "Just say thank you."

"Say thank you for what?" McKinley looked at him confused.

"Look." He pointed toward the window.

McKinley looked out the window and realized that they were no longer taking off, but in the air, surrounded by a sea of clouds.

"Now say thank you." Koran placed his head back, closed his eyes and smiled.

"I wish I would." McKinley rolled her eyes.

"That's cool. Don't ask me for help no more."

"I didn't in the first place." She folded her arms across her chest.

Thirty minutes later, after sitting in silence and trying their best to pretend that the other didn't exist, the sky had gone from blue to gray. A heavy thunderstorm had formed and was causing the plane to experience a lot of turbulence.

McKinley stopped a flight attendant as she made her way down the aisle. "What's happening?"

"It's just a little turbulence. Everything will be fine," the flight attendant assured with a smile, trying her best not to fall.

McKinley panicked. "Why is this happening to me?"

"Didn't you just hear what the flight attendant just said?" Koran asked. "Everything's gon' be straight."

But as soon as the words came out of his mouth the plane shook violently, causing the yellow oxygen masks to fall from the ceiling.

"This is your captain speaking, ladies and gentlemen. I may have underestimated the storm just a tad bit. But I'm afraid we are being diverted to Jacksonville Airport, as Atlanta International Airport has been shut down. Once we land, the staff will be happy to book you onto connecting flights, in order to get you to your final destination."

"I told you." McKinley began to cry. "We're all going to die!" She screamed, "Jesus, take me now!"

"I'd rather argue wit'
you than to be with
someone else."

Kanye West feat
John Legend and
Chris Rock "Blame
Game"

The main terminal of Jacksonville Airport was filled with enraged and shaken-up passengers trying to figure out how they were going to get to their destinations. Among the slew of people was McKinley. After sitting and waiting three hours for a seat on a plane, she bombarded her way through the crowd with her purse in hand. Although it had been said repeatedly that all flights were canceled due to inclement weather, she was determined to find a way out of Hicksville, USA and fast.

She questioned an elderly woman behind the service desk. "So are you telling me that there are absolutely no flights leaving out of here until tomorrow?

"Nope," the woman said, not even bothering to look up.

"None?" McKinley said in disbelief.

The woman looked up at her. "I believe that's what I said the first time."

"Well, see," McKinley looked at the woman's name tag, "Cricket, I have a huge problem with that, 'cause I need to get home today."

"So does everybody else, Prima Donna."

McKinley frowned at the woman and turned around pissed. She was even more upset to find that Koran was sitting right behind her and had overheard everything.

She screwed up her face. "What the hell are you laughing at?"

"Nothing." He chuckled.

"I swear this is some bullshit."

She didn't know how her life could get any worse. Her man, who was really somebody else's man, was dead. She was broke, homeless and stranded in a city where it looked like the local Wal-Mart was the hippest place in town.

"Mr. McKnight, your car is ready," a Hertz representative said to Koran.

Koran stood up, gathered his things and walked over to the Hertz station to pick up his keys. McKinley watched him eagerly like a fat kid who was dying for the last piece of cake. Sure she'd been a bitch to him all morning, but there was no way she could allow him to leave without taking her with him.

"Koran," she called out.

Koran stopped mid-stride and smiled to himself. Before turning around, he erased the smile off of his face.

"What?" he asked with an attitude.

"I assume you're driving back to St. Louis?"

"You would assume right."

"Look, I know we've had our moments, but is there any way I could ride back with you?"

He shook his head. "I don't know about that."

"Why not? I promise I won't even bother you. Hell, I won't even talk to you if you don't want me to."

"Put that on something." Koran twisted his lips to the side, not believing her.

"I put that on everything," she lied.

"Cool, but I'ma need one more thing from you."

"What?" McKinley eyed him quizzically.

Koran stepped into her personal space. "A kiss."

"You out yo' damn mind," McKinley scoffed.

"A'ight, stay yo' ass here then." Koran began to walk away.

"Really?" she challenged.

"Yeah." Koran looked at her.

"This is not right." McKinley approached him.

"You either gon' do it or you ain't," Koran replied.

Knowing she had no other choice but to either put up or shut up, McKinley wrapped her arms around his neck and gave him the most sensuous kiss he'd ever had. Right there in the middle of the airport their lips and tongues intertwined.

"Are you happy now?" McKinley asked, stepping back.

"I mean, yeah. I just asked for a peck, you ain't have to put ya' tongue all in my mouth." Koran twisted up his face, pretending as if he hadn't enjoyed every second of it.

"Whatever. Can we go now?" McKinley rolled her eyes.

"Yeah, but if you get out of line one more time yo' ass is out."

She raised her right arm and saluted him. "I promise I'll behave. Scout's honor."

XoXo

Relieved that she finally had a way home, McKinley walked into the revolving door and outside to the roaring, windy thunderstorm. McKinley dropped her head low and tried her best to conceal herself, but to no affect. The wind was so forceful that she couldn't even walk at a normal pace or stand straight. She tried calling out for Koran who was ahead of her, but every time she went to open her mouth, a sea of water would choke her.

After what seemed like a five-mile walk, they finally made it to the car, which was a bright yellow 2011 PT Cruiser. McKinley couldn't believe her eyes. This had to have been some kind of sick joke. No way was this the rental car. McKinley was so taken aback by the vehicle that she didn't even hear Koran calling out her name.

"McKinley," he shouted once again, holding onto to the hood of the trunk.

"Huh?" She blinked her eyes, coming back to reality.

"The door is open," he shouted.

Nodding her head, McKinley got inside the car with a bewildered expression on her face. Drenched, she slowly placed on her seatbelt while wondering if this was all a bad dream. The car was so bright it made her head hurt.

"Whew." Koran sighed, wiping the drops of rain from his face.

McKinley looked at him. "This is a joke, right?"

"Is what a joke?" Koran asked perplexed.

"This car." She looked around.

"I know it's brighter than a muthafucka, but it's the only thing they had left. It was either this or a yellow Bug."

"I will be so glad when I see the *Welcome to Missouri* sign, so this trip from hell can be over with," McKinley replied.

"That's like the second thing you've said all day that I've agreed with." Koran started up the engine, only for it to cut off seconds later.

"Now what do you have to say, Big Mouth?" McKinley folded her arms across her chest.

"Didn't we agree, no talkin'?" Koran turned the key again.

This time the car cranked up right away without any problem.

"It ain't my fault you fell for that shit." McKinley giggled.

"Whatever. You just sit back and look pretty. I got this."

"Uh huh." McKinley pursed her lips, trying her best not to smile.

Koran was a cutie pie, but he was arrogant as hell. From the little that she could remember about their night of passion, his sex game wasn't too shabby either. But what could a one-night stand lead to? It wasn't like they were going to fall madly in love and ride off into the sunset and live happily ever after. She reminded herself of the reasons why they wouldn't work:

1. They barely knew each other.
2. He could be crazy.
3. He might have a hint of beat-a-bitch down in him.
4. He could very well already have a woman.
5. He could have fifty million kids spread around the United States.
6. He could be crazy!

Besides that, McKinley was still mourning the death of Jamil. The wounds of his death and betrayal hadn't even begun to heal. Plus, what honestly did she have to offer a dog, let alone a fine, strong, cocky-ass man like Koran? She needed to get herself in order before she could jump into anything. Needing to hear something inspirational, McKinley leaned forward and turned the radio station from the FM Hip Hop and R&B station Koran was playing to an AM gospel station.

"Another Day's Journey" by LaShun Pace was playing. McKinley gazed out of the window and tapped her foot while singing along.

"I got my health and strength y'all—"

Koran switched the station back to the FM side.

McKinley shot him a look that could kill and switched it back to AM.

"A lil Jesus never hurt nobody," she said.

"And neither did a lil' Jay-Z." Koran pushed her hand away and turned the knob once more.

Determined to beat him at his own game, McKinley pinched him in the arm and switched the knob back to LaShun Pace.

"Oww, that shit hurt!" Koran yanked his arm up and down then quickly turned the station.

"OOOOOOOOOH!" McKinley mockingly groaned, forcefully turning the knob back, but this time causing it to break off.

"Look at what you did!" She held the knob up. "Now neither of us can listen to the radio."

Koran pulled over to the side of the road. "Get out!"

"What?" McKinley looked at him like he was crazy.

"Get out!"

"You're kidding me?"

"Does it look like I'm playin' wit' you? Get out!" Koran reached over her and opened the passenger side door.

"I can't get out and walk. I have on Chanel heels." She pouted.

"Oh, yes you can, and you will." Koran unbuckled her seatbelt.

"But I'm sorry." McKinley poked out her bottom lip.

"No, you're not."

"Yes, I am." McKinley smiled and nodded her head simultaneously.

"Sorry for what?" Koran inquired.

"I'm sorry I broke the knob."

"What else?"

McKinley held her head down and whispered, "I'm sorry I turned the station without asking."

"You're missing something."

"I'm sorry I spoke out loud." She rolled her eyes.

"Thank you. That's better. Now close your door," Koran ordered while making his way back onto the road.

Part Three

*"No one has to know
what you are feeling, no
one but me and you."*

Alicia Keys

"Diary"

"No, no!" McKinley shook from side to side while asleep. "No, Jamil! Jamil!" she screamed, jumping out of her sleep, scaring Koran half to death.

"Oh, my God!" She inhaled and exhaled.

"What the fuck is wrong wit' you?" Koran asked, trying his best to stay focused on the road.

"Nothin'." McKinley panted, holding her chest.

"I don't know about you, but to me that was something."

"I said it was nothin'," McKinley insisted, wiping her face with her hands.

"Then who is Jamil?" Koran quizzed.

McKinley snapped her neck to the side and looked at him. "What did you just say?"

"I said who is Jamil?" Koran replied, bluntly.

"Nobody." McKinley leaned back.

"He must be somebody, you over there dreaming about him," Koran replied back.

"Will you mind yo' damn business? He's nobody. Now can you stop at the next exit? I have to pee, or is that up for discussion, too?"

By the expression on her face, Koran could tell that he'd overstepped his boundaries. Instead of putting her in her place for talkin' slick, Koran did as he was asked and got off of the highway. A Shell station was down the road, so he stopped there. He wasn't even parked well at a pump before McKinley jumped out and slammed the door behind her.

Inside the restroom, McKinley turned on the faucet and let the cool water run over her hands. Relishing the sensation, she splashed the soothing water onto her face.

After grabbing a paper towel and drying her face off, McKinley gazed at herself in the mirror. Ever since Jamil died, she'd had trouble sleeping. Most nights she stayed awake as long as she could in fear of the nightmares she was sure to have. McKinley just wanted her life to get back to normal. But what about her life was normal? She was taking a road trip home with a complete stranger whom she'd had a one-night stand with the night before.

Thinking of Koran made McKinley feel horrible. He was only trying to figure out what was wrong with her and she'd completely gone off on him. Not liking what she saw staring back at her in the mirror, McKinley walked out of the restroom. Koran stood at the side of the car, pumping gas, when he noticed every time he looked at her the hairs on his arm stood up. She was petite compared to Whitney, but her face and dimples were the exact same. She seemed to have been dropped down from heaven. He knew McKinley probably thought he was weird for randomly staring at her all the time, but he couldn't take his eyes off of her.

The only way he could tell McKinley and Whitney apart was by their personalities. Whitney was far more gentle and soft-spoken. Not to say she didn't know how to get rowdy when necessary. Koran missed his wife terribly. Thoughts of her caused his heart to ache. He'd give anything to have her back in his arms again and to be there to see their daughter grow. But no matter how much he wished and prayed, his prayers weren't going to come true.

Tank filled, Koran got back into the car and started the engine. On the road again, he and McKinley sat quietly.

Unable to bear the silence, McKinley began to talk. "I'm sorry for snapping on you like that."

"It's cool."

"No, it's not." She looked down at her hands. Tears were starting to slowly form in her eyes. "My life is a mess." McKinley began to cry.

Koran looked over at her. "You, a'ight?" he asked, concerned.

"No." She wiped her eyes. "A couple of weeks ago, my fiancé was killed."

"Damn, for real? That's fucked up," Koran said sincerely.

"Tell me about it," McKinley agreed. "I didn't even get to go to the funeral."

"Why?"

"'Cause he was married." McKinley cried even harder.

"What?" Koran said, shocked.

"After he died, I found out that he'd been living a double life. The whole three years we were together, he had a whole wife, kids and a whole 'nother chick on the side and my dumbass didn't even know it. I mean, how gullible could I possibly be? I had no clue."

"That's some deep shit," Koran said, overwhelmed by her confession.

"Since he passed my whole life has been turned upside down. All I knew was him. He was my everything. My whole life was centered around him."

"Well, see, that's where you fucked up."

"What?" She blew her nose on a napkin.

"I don't give a fuck how much you love a man; never make him your whole world. That's where y'all females fuck up."

"Thanks for making me feel even worse." McKinley chuckled.

"My bad. I wasn't tryin' to be mean or nothin'. I'm just statin' facts." Koran shrugged.

"If you say so."

"Nah, for real. I'm sorry for your loss. It's a fucked-up feeling losing someone you love. No matter what the circumstances are," Koran said somberly. "I know that shit gotta hurt," he continued.

"Like hell," she agreed.

"So that's why you were in tears yesterday?"

"How did you know I'd been cryin'?" McKinley asked,

surprised.

"'Cause your eyes were red and you looked like you'd lost your favorite Chanel bag or something," Koran teased.

"You stupid." McKinley laughed.

"I'm serious. I was like 'Damn, let me go give this girl a hug before she have to be put on suicide watch,'" he teased.

"I did look pitiful, didn't I?" McKinley sniffled.

"You said it. I didn't." Koran chuckled.

"It's cool. I know I did."

"On the real though," Koran said, "I understand that you're hurting now, and the pain will last for a while, but eventually things will get better. One day you're going to wake up and it's not going to hurt as bad. The pain will go from a throbbing sensation to just a little sting."

"How do you know so much about mourning someone's death?"

"My mother died of an overdose when I was a teenager."

"Wow. I'm sorry," McKinley said, flabbergasted.

"It's all good," he assured.

"Death is never good. You can say how you really feel around me."

"I mean, I felt abandoned, but I did what I had to do to survive."

"Like what?"

"I sold dope, but a good friend of mine helped me realize

that wasn't the route to go, so I stopped."

"What do you do now?"

"I own a couple of businesses back home."

"That's good. Most dudes don't ever stop. Case and point, my fiancé."

"Yeah, well, I had reasons outside of my control that got me out the game." Koran thought back to Whitney's illness and the birth of his daughter.

"Really? What?"

"Ay, you hungry?" Koran asked, changing the subject.

"Always." McKinley grinned.

"Let's grab something to eat. All of this talkin' has made me hungry."

"Okay." She smiled, genuinely enjoying his company.

"I'm here as long as you
need me"
Brandy
"All In Me"

For the next two hours McKinley and Koran laughed and talked about everything from childhood memories and favorite restaurants to their top five MC's. On the surface, things were cool, but underlying emotions from the night before and untold details from their lives stayed stuck on pause in their throat.

"How can you not respect Kanye?" Koran asked, amped.

"Ever since I saw him rock a leopard-print shirt, his ass been a lil' suspect to me. I'm tellin' you, that negro got *How you doing?* written all over him." McKinley flicked her wrist.

"Get the fuck outta here." Koran laughed, yawning. "So what did you do for a living back in Miami?"

"Umm," McKinley stammered. She couldn't just come out and say nothing. It would make her look like a bird. "I was a personal shopper," she lied.

"That's what's up." Koran nodded his head. "Yo, I'm gettin' tired. I think we need to get a room for the night and start fresh in the morning." He looked over at her. "I saw a sign for a Marriot hotel a couple of miles back, so it should be coming up soon."

McKinley panicked. "I'll drive. I'm not tired."

If she had to tell Koran that she was broke on top of everything she'd already revealed, she'd die of embarrassment.

"Please, you've been over there yawning yo' ass off. Ain't no way in hell I'ma let you behind this wheel," he declared.

"I promise you, I'm good," McKinley protested.

"Nah, we both need to rest. Plus, I could use a bath, so I know you got to be dying for one, too."

"What you tryin' to say?" McKinley cocked her head back.

"Fall back," Koran laughed, getting off the highway. "I ain't tryin' to say nothin'. I'm sayin' you need to wash yo' ass," he joked.

McKinley ignored his sarcasm. "But what if it's a nasty Marriot with dingy carpeting and a moldy smell?"

"Does this look like a dingy Marriot to you?" Koran asked, pulling into the parking lot.

McKinley looked up at the building. Koran was right. It was a nice hotel. The Marriot hotel in Knoxville, Tennessee was on a hilltop overlooking the Tennessee River. *Dammit*, McKinley thought. She had to find a way out of this somehow. In a last ditch effort to change Koran's mind, she said, "I really feel uneasy about this. Something in my spirit is just sayin' this ain't right."

"Chill out. Everything's going to be fine. From the looks of it, this has to be at least a four-star hotel. Now come on." Koran got out of the car and popped the trunk.

With only one more option left McKinley grabbed her purse from the back seat of the car and got out as well. As Koran strolled into the hotel, McKinley lagged behind him slowly. At the service desk Koran paid for his room.

"Have a wonderful night, sir." The front desk clerk smiled.

"You, too." Koran smiled back, taking his key.

"You know what?" McKinley slapped her hand against her forehead. "I think I left something in the car. Let me get the keys, so I can run back and go get it."

"Here." Koran tossed her the keys. "You want me to wait on you?"

"No, go ahead up to your room. I'll be fine," she assured as the elevator doors opened.

"A'ight." Koran turned and hopped inside.

As the doors to the elevator closed, McKinley let out a sigh of relief. Swiftly, she walked back to the car, got in and locked the doors. For the first time that day she'd dodged a bullet successfully. She could've come out and told him the truth, but the truth was that McKinley was ashamed. She was ashamed that she'd allowed herself to be put in this position. For the last three years of her life, she'd enjoyed the perks of dating a rich man, only to be left with nothing but designer tags.

The only sort of achievement she'd made in life thus far was mastering the art of a sample sale. Her pride was just too strong to let Koran know that she was penniless. She respected him and wanted him to respect her, too. Her life was already in shambles. The last thing she needed was Koran looking down at her.

"McKinley!" Koran tapped on the passenger side window,

causing her to jump.

"Huh?" She stared up at him.

"What are you doing?"

"Umm," she tried to think of a lie. "I was lookin' for my lipstick." She smiled.

"Open the door," Koran insisted.

McKinley unlocked the door, knowing she'd been caught.

"Now are you gon' tell me the truth or do I have to pry it out of you?"

McKinley gazed off to the side. She felt like a little kid who'd been caught with her hand in the cookie jar.

"I don't have any money," she finally said.

"You're broke?" Koran asked, surprised.

"Yeah, like broke, broke. After Jamil died, the Feds froze all of my accounts. All I have is the money in my pocket, which is nothing but twenty dollars. My mother and best friend had to pay for my airline ticket home." Her lips trembled.

"Who are you?" Koran eyed her suspiciously. "I mean, is your name even McKinley?"

"See, this is why I didn't wanna tell you." McKinley tried to close the door, but Koran stopped her by pulling it back open.

"What?" she whined.

"What do you really think you're doing?"

"I don't know."

"Look, even though you're a walkin', talkin' Lifetime movie, you can sleep in my room."

She shook her head. "You don't have to do that."

"I know I don't." He winked his eye.

After riding the elevator up to the third floor, Koran and McKinley entered room 315. McKinley was pleasantly surprised at how clean and chic the room was. On the bed there was a brand-new down comforter and fluffy white pillows. Instead of using hotel bath soaps, they used Bath and Body Works products. Worn out from the day, McKinley kicked off her heels. Her feet were killing her. Unbeknownst to McKinley, while she stretched her toes, Koran had started to strip down.

"Oh my God, you were right. I didn't even realize until now how tired I was." She yawned. "I just thought about it though. I don't have anything to put on."

"Here, you can wear one of my T-shirts." Koran threw one at her.

McKinley turned around to catch it and noticed that Koran had nothing on but a pair of boxer briefs.

"What the hell?" she yelled.

"What's wrong wit' you?" He rummaged through his suitcase for something to sleep in.

"Umm, dude, you couldn't go in the bathroom and change?" McKinley shielded her eyes with her hand. She prayed to God he couldn't see how red her face was.

"It ain't like you ain't never seen me naked before." Koran took off his underwear and walked passed her.

McKinley couldn't risk taking a peek. Koran's ass was so firm you could bounce a quarter off of it. McKinley wasn't even aware how hard she was staring at him until he spun around unexpectedly. His ten-inch dick was staring her smack dab in the face. His dick was surely something she'd forgotten during their drunken tryst.

How she could've erased that from her memory was beyond her, because his dick was a mouthwatering sight to see. It was long and thick and the tip reminded her of a tootsie roll Blow Pop that she wanted to suck all of the flavor out of.

"McKinley!" Koran shouted, getting her attention.

"Huh?" She blinked her eyes.

"You mind ordering some room service?" Koran asked, knowing damn well his body was causing her to go into convulsions.

Once the order was placed, McKinley retrieved her cell phone and called her mother to let her know she was okay. By the time she ended the call, Koran was coming out of the bathroom. McKinley tried to act like he didn't have any effect on her as she grabbed her things and walked past him, but her eyes kept gravitating to the bulge in his underwear. The cup could barely hold his dick, it was so big.

Needing to get herself together, McKinley scurried into the bathroom and closed the door behind her. With her back against the door, she wondered would she be able to stay in the same room with Koran without taking every inch of his manhood in her mouth. *I mean, ain't nothin' wrong wit' a lil bump and grind,* she thought. Deciding it was best she take a cold shower, McKinley turned on the water and got naked.

The cold water was freezing, but it helped get her mind in order. She couldn't continue to let Koran take her off her game. She had to stay focused on the task at hand, which was getting home in one piece and figuring out her life from then on. Fresh and clean, McKinley stepped out of the shower. Minutes later, she dried off, lathered on lotion and slipped on the T-shirt Koran had given her.

The shirt barely covered her ass cheeks, but it would have to do because she had no other options. It was, however, the first time McKinley wished she wore panties. Gathering her clothes, she opened the door. The first thing she noticed was Koran sitting on the edge of the bed, eating the juiciest burger she'd ever seen. Upon sight, her stomach instantly growled. She was mortified. The sound was so loud that even Koran heard it.

"Did you just fart?" He scrunched up his forehead, disgusted.

"No. That was my stomach." Her cheeks turned beet red.

"Yeah, okay." Koran scrunched up his face and continued chewing. "Your food is over there on the table." He gestured with his head.

"Thanks," McKinley replied, folding her clothes as quickly as possible.

The smell of the burger was driving her mad. McKinley didn't even bother to sit down. She simply popped off the lid and devoured the bacon cheeseburger right there on the spot. A bit of juice from the meat trickled down her chin, but she didn't care. Her stomach was saying, "Feed me, bitch." McKinley was eating so fast that Koran stopped eating his food and sat back and watched her in awe.

Full and exhausted from the long day they'd endured; McKinley and Koran slipped underneath the covers and lay down. Both made sure to lie as far away from the other as possible. Although being in such close proximity to each other was making both of their temperatures rise. Koran lay on his back, gazing up at the ceiling. He'd never once in his life lay beside a woman in bed and not touch her.

McKinley was so close to him that he could reach out and touch her, but he didn't want to invade her personnel space. Instead of acting on impulse, Koran swung his legs out of the bed and sat up. His muscular back faced McKinley as he glided his hands over his head and down his face. McKinley watched him in awe. So many erotic thoughts bombarded her mind, she couldn't think straight.

With every blink of the eye and movement of her body, she yearned for him. All she could imagine was him lying on top of her and caressing her thighs. Her body needed him in the worst way. Nervous as hell, McKinley crawled over to his side of the bed and wrapped her arms around his neck.

"What you doing, man?" Koran asked, relishing the feel of her tongue on his earlobe.

"Exactly what you want me to do." McKinley placed a trail of light kisses from his ear to his cheek.

"You sure you wanna do this?"

"Mmm hmm." McKinley ran her hand down his chest.

She then strategically slipped her hand inside his boxers and began massaging his rock-hard dick. Turned on to the fullest, Koran turned his face to the side and stared at her. McKinley was beautiful, and if he made love to her he wasn't going to hold anything back. Figuring they were two consenting adults who knew exactly what they were getting themselves into, he gently cupped McKinley's face with his hands and kissed her lips. As their tongues intertwined, McKinley found herself drowning with every touch of his hand. Koran felt the same exact way. Laying on top of her, he swiftly ran his hand up her shirt and toyed with her nipples.

With every stroke of his fingers, McKinley's temperature rose. Koran stared into her big brown eyes. McKinley was beautiful. Her voluptuous physique melted his heart. Koran couldn't wait to enter her wet slit again. She was so warm, he could stay there forever. Knowing exactly what was on his mind, McKinley parted her legs.

She had to have him. The need for him to be inside of her grew with each second. All she could think about were his deep kisses and his strong hands massaging her breasts while he grinded in and out of her at a feverish pace.

Always one to please, Koran slipped his manhood into her warm hole. The feeling was sensational.

McKinley held onto his back and willed herself not to come. She wanted this moment to last forever. Being with Koran sexually was unlike anything she'd ever experienced before. He took his time with her. He made sure she felt every stroke, every bite, every lick of his tongue. That night, underneath the light of the pale moon, their bodies twisted against each other in slow ecstasy. Flesh to flesh, they consumed one another until both their desires were met and neither could go anymore.

"She can't see in me what I see in her."

Wale feat Marsha Ambrosius

"Diary"

"You ready?" Koran asked the next morning.

"Yep." McKinley looked at him then turned her head.

The first time they'd slept together both were in a drunken stupor. The next morning memories of each touch, kiss and thrust was clouded. But last night they both were fully aware. Their bodies had become one in the most erotic way. Now, as they resumed their road trip home, both wondered if they had made the right decision by taking it there, because now there was no turning back. They couldn't blame their actions on the alcohol. Every moan, whimper and scream had come from the most sacred place inside their hearts.

For a while they both rode in silence, too afraid to speak what was on their minds. Instead of talking, Koran and McKinley took in the scenic view. Nothing but acres of grass filled with corn and sugar cane surrounded them. Inside the car, Koran and McKinley began to hear a popping sound come from the engine.

"Oh, my God! What is that?" McKinley sat up, frightened.

"The engine." Koran rode along the rode cautiously.

"Why is it making that noise?" McKinley's voice shook slightly.

"Like I know."

McKinley panicked. "Please tell me that's not smoke."

"Where?" Koran said, alarmed.

McKinley pointed. "The hood!"

"Fuck!" Koran hit the steering wheel, heated.

"Lord, help me! We're gettin' ready to die. And I didn't even get to see Beyoncé live in concert," McKinley screeched.

Koran tried his best to continue down the road, but sputtering noises, loud pops that sounded like gunshots, and smoke coming from the engine made him realize he had no choice but to stop.

"Why are you pulling over?"

"'Cause I think the transmission's gone out." Koran turned off the engine and got out.

"Oh my God! You have got to be fuckin' kidding me." McKinley placed her head back against the headrest and closed her eyes. "This cannot be happening to me."

"Fuck!" Koran slammed the hood shut.

"C'mon, man, we gon' have to walk." He took the keys out of the ignition.

McKinley looked at him like he was crazy. "Excuse you? These shoes ain't made for walkin'."

"Well, I don't know what to tell you. I'm gettin' ready to walk until I find something." Koran took his luggage out of the trunk.

"We're in the middle of nowhere. Do you know how long that could be?" McKinley yelled out of the window.

"I don't care. I'm not staying here," Koran yelled over his

shoulder as he walked with his baggage in tow.

"Well, I'm not walkin' no damn where." McKinley folded her arms across her chest. "What the hell I look like?"

But as McKinley looked around at the acres of land and thought about what could possibly be lurking around in it, she became overwhelmingly scared. Realizing that she had no other choice but to walk, she grabbed her purse and got out of the car.

"Wait on me!" She jogged toward Koran.

"I thought you would come to your senses," he teased.

She pushed him in the arm. "Shut up."

Two hours into their hike, McKinley's feet were on fire. Her feet hurt so bad she walked with a limp. She was almost sure she had a blister or two on her feet as well. Koran felt bad for her. He would've gladly picked her up and carried her, but he had his luggage to pull.

"I can't do this much longer," McKinley whined as tears poured from her eyes.

"I know, baby." Koran stopped walking and helped her ease her way down to the ground to sit.

McKinley's heart skipped a beat. She hadn't expected for Koran to call her baby.

"What are we gonna do?" She tried her best not to blush.

"I think I see something up the road. Look, you just stay here and rest and watch my bags. I'll be back as soon as I can."

"Uh ah." McKinley's eyes grew wide. "You ain't gon' leave me out here in the wilderness for some crazy ass to come out of the woodworks and come kill me. No, no. I'll walk some more if I have to."

"No, you won't and you can't. I promise I'll be back in less than an hour. I'ma run there and back."

McKinley inhaled deeply. After dealing with Jamil, and his unreliability, she had a hard time trusting Koran's word, but something in his eyes told her that he was telling the truth. "Okay, but hurry back."

"I will." Koran kissed her on the forehead before running off.

McKinley watched Koran until his back faded. Alone and a little afraid, she took off her heels and massaged her red, aching and swollen feet. Every now and then she'd hear something rattle in the wind that caused her to jump. But for the most part, McKinley was able to keep her cool. That was until she saw something big, brown and furry traipsing across the field.

"Oh my God! It's Big Foot." She got up off the ground to get a better view of the huge creature. "Yeah, that's most definitely Big Foot," she panicked. "I see now I'ma have to fuck Big Foot up." She picked up her heel, ready to strike.

But it wasn't Big Foot. McKinley's fear and wild imagination had gotten the best of her. What she thought was Big

Foot was really only a wolf. The wolf, however, was now only a few feet away from her. This was it. McKinley was scared shitless, but she wasn't about to go down without a fight. Just as the wolf was nearing, Koran came zooming down the road in a pick-up truck driven by an older white man. Thankfully, the speed and un-expectancy of the truck scared the wolf away.

"Hallelujah, thank You, Jesus!" McKinley rushed over into Koran's arms. "Did you see it?" she asked terrified.

"See what?" He held her close.

McKinley pointed. "The half-man, half-wolf. It was just over there in the field."

Koran hung his head and smiled. "Yo, I think you been out in the sun too long."

"I'm not crazy. One of the wolves from *Twilight* was about to make me his dinner."

"Aww shucks, that wasn't nothin' but an ol' stray dog," the older white gentleman said.

"Who the hell is that?" McKinley whispered to Koran.

"McKinley, this kind man is Bobby Joe. He and his lovely wife, Jodeen, owns the Quickie Mart down the road, and would you believe that on top of the Quickie Mart is a room?" Koran said, excited.

"That's wonderful," McKinley responded dryly.

"Well, grab your things and let's get a move on," Bobby Joe said. "*Nash Bridges* is about to come on."

"You ain't got to tell me twice." McKinley scurried and grabbed her things and got into the truck.

Koran threw his bags in the back of the truck and hopped into the front seat next to McKinley. Bobby Joe then started up the engine and they all rode down the street, making small talk.

"So how long you two lovebirds been married?" Bobby Joe questioned.

"Uh, we're not—" McKinley uttered.

Koran cut her off. "Almost a year."

"Newlyweds, huh? Oh, I remember those days. Me and the missus have been married for over thirty years," Bobby Joe said proudly.

"Really?" McKinley looked over at Koran with an expression on her face that said, "When the hell did we get married?"

"Just play along," he mouthed.

"Here we are. Home sweet home." Bobby Joe pulled in front of the store.

"Koran, here are the keys. You and the missus can let yourselves in around the back. If you need anything, just come into the store and holler. If you need anything after store hours, our farmhouse is right down the road, next to the bait shop."

"Thank you very much, Bobby Joe." Koran shook his hand.

"Yeah, thank you, Bobby Joe." McKinley smiled.

Koran used the key and unlocked the door to the room. It was just like he'd imagined it to be, small and quaint. Only the basics were in the room. There was a queen-sized bed, a nightstand with a rotary phone on top, a dresser and an old television with an antenna.

"Now why are we married again?" McKinley asked, sitting on the edge of the bed.

"Bobby Joe and his wife only rent out the room to married couples, so I told him what he wanted to hear, so we could have a place to stay tonight."

"Well, in that case, hubby, can I use your phone, 'cause my battery went out?" McKinley batted her eyes.

"Yeah, here." Koran handed her his phone. "I'm getting ready to get in the shower."

"Can I join you?" McKinley arched her eyebrow.

"I don't play that teasing shit. If you gon' do something just do it."

"I just might." McKinley winked her eye.

"Yeah, a'ight, we'll see." Koran dug into his bag and pulled out a fresh pair of underwear and clothes before heading into the shower.

McKinley called her mother.

Her mother answered on the first ring. "Hello?"

"Hi, Ma."

"McKinley, where are you?" Her mother's voice rose. "I've been callin' your phone all morning."

"I'm in Tennessee. The transmission went out."

"So when will you be home now?" her mother questioned.

"I guess in the next day or so. We're going to take the train now," McKinley explained.

"Where are y'all staying?"

"Koran rented us out a room."

"Okay, well call me tonight before you go to bed, so I can make sure you're alright."

"I will," McKinley assured as someone clicked onto the line. "Mama, I gotta click over. I'll call you later. Hello?"

"Hello?" a little girl said back.

"Hello?" McKinley said again.

"Hello?"

"Hello?" McKinley said once more, taken aback.

"Helloooooooo?" the little girl sang.

"Okay, who is this?" McKinley asked with an attitude.

"Harlow. Is my daddy there?"

"Your *daddy?*" McKinley said, taken aback.

"Yeah."

"Harlow, who is that?" a woman in the background asked.

"I don't know. I'm just lookin' for my daddy."

"Hand me the phone," the woman said.

Remembering what had happened with Jamil, McKinley didn't even bother speaking to the woman. Instead, she quickly hung up. It was like life was repeating itself all over again. She'd fallen once more for a man who led a secret life. Her life couldn't get any worse. She felt like a complete and utter fool. Tears flooded her eyes. McKinley swallowed hard. She was so caught up in her emotions that she hadn't even realized that the shower had stopped running and Koran had stepped back into the room.

"I guess you must've changed your mind?" he said, securing the towel around his waist.

"Fuck you!" she spat, throwing the phone at his chest.

"What the fuck is wrong wit' you?" Koran caught the phone mid-air.

"You!" she shrieked. "The damn broke-down plane. The fucked-up car, this dump." She swung her arms in the air. "Jamil's two-faced ass, that's what's wrong," McKinley snapped, picking up her shoes and purse.

"Where you going?" Koran asked, still perplexed.

"Anywhere but here," McKinley shouted, slamming the door behind her.

Unaware of where her sudden change in demeanor came from, Koran threw on his clothes and followed her. He found her sitting outside on the steps in the back of the building.

Koran sat down next to her. "What the hell is your problem?"

"Why didn't you tell me you were married?" McKinley sniffled.

"What are you talkin' about?" he questioned, confused.

"While I was on the phone with my mother your other line clicked and I answered it." McKinley took a much-needed breath. "And some lil' girl was on the line, then your wife got on the phone. And all I could think about was what happened with me and Jamil and I just felt so stupid. Like, how could I have not learned my lesson the first time?" She sobbed. "You're way too fine to be single."

"First of all, I'm not married." Koran chuckled. "I mean, I am, but I'm not."

"Huh?" McKinley gazed up at him, perplexed.

"That must've been my daughter's nanny who got on the phone."

"So you *do* have a kid?" McKinley's heart dropped down to her knees.

"Yeah. I do." Koran nodded his head.

"Why didn't you tell me?"

"'Cause I didn't know you that well and I didn't feel like I had to," he stated matter-of-factly. "Real talk, ever since my daughter was born it's been just me and her. Her mother, my wife, Whitney, died after giving birth to her. She had cancer." Koran's voice trailed off.

"Koran, I am so sorry."

"It's cool."

"No, it's not. I am such an idiot." McKinley slapped her hand against her forehead. "Will you please forgive me?"

"You're forgiven, crybaby." Koran hugged her around her neck.

"But what I wanna know is where did you really think you were going?" He laughed.

"I don't know." She laughed, too.

"You crazy, but look, come with me." Koran stood up and wiped off the back of his pants.

"Where are we going?" McKinley asked, confused.

"Just come with me." He extended his hand.

"Have you forgotten that my feet are all swole?" McKinley extended her legs.

"Just come on." Koran pulled her up and drug her around to the front of the store.

Koran pulled the store's door open. The Quickie Mart was one of those stores that sold some of everything. They carried tires, fabric, bread, clothes, tools, you name it and you could find it.

"So this is your wife?" Jodeen smiled, coming from behind the counter. Jodeen was a dead ringer for Paula Deen. Her hair was a sparkling silver shade, just like hers, and her baby-blue eyes lit up like the sky. "She's even prettier than you described." Jodeen smiled at McKinley, cheerfully.

"Thank you." McKinley beamed.

"What can I do for you?" Jodeen spoke with a country twang.

"My wife lost her luggage," Koran began to explain.

"Poor dear," Jodeen clasped her hands together.

"So we need to pick up a few things for her to wear," Koran continued.

"You say what now?" McKinley cocked her head back.

"I have the perfect outfit." Jodeen cheerfully rushed over to the clothing section, which consisted of Dickies and John Deer.

"Everything in here is one hundred percent polyester," McKinley whispered. "If I'm even near polyester my skin breaks out."

"I'm tired of seeing you in this outfit, so you gon' have to do something," Koran declared.

"Here we are." Jodeen held up a pair of Dickies overalls. "Isn't it lovely?"

"Oh, it's special all right." McKinley's upper lip curled.

"She'll take it," Koran chimed in.

"Whenever I'm alone
with you, you make me feel
like I am whole again."

Adele

"Lovesong"

For the rest of the day, McKinley and Koran enjoyed each other's presence while lying in bed. They talked, slept and even made love again, but when the sun began to fall and their stomachs began to growl, they knew it was time to get up. The bar across the street was the quickest place to get to on foot, so they headed over.

Trudy's Place was like something out of a movie. Everything from the tables to the jukebox was made of wood. On the walls were deer heads and old John Wayne posters. Outside of themselves, only three other black people were in the spot, but Koran and McKinley didn't care. They were on a mission to eat and have a good time. The next morning, they would be boarding a train back to St. Louis.

While waiting on Koran to return with their beer and wings, McKinley scratched her arms and legs profusely. She absolutely detested the wife beater, overalls and tan-colored Timberland boots she wore. The rough and cheap fabric was driving her nuts. Other than that, she was having a wonderful time.

"Here you go, pretty girl." Koran sat her mug of beer down before her.

"Thank you. Ooh, these wings look yummy." McKinley rubbed her hands together, excited.

"Right, I'm hungrier than a muthafucka." Koran took a seat across from her.

"Yo, I swear to God I feel like I'm in the *Twilight Zone*." McKinley looked around the bar in awe. "I've only seen people like this on the *Simple Life* and *Toddlers and Tiaras*."

Koran cracked up laughing. "I know you got some family from the south. Every black person does," he said.

"Yeah, but this shit right here is a whole 'nother ballgame." McKinley laughed, causing Koran to laugh, too.

"You know, you look kinda cute in them bibs. You might need to come on up outta them when we get back to the room." He winked his eye.

"Oh, really, and what's gon' happen when I take 'em off?"

"I'ma do what Lloyd said and lay it down."

"You so whack." McKinley laughed with glee.

Once they were done eating, McKinley and Koran played a game of pool and darts. McKinley wasn't very good at either, but Koran took the time to show her different techniques. Then the music slowed down and couples hit the dance floor.

"You wanna dance?" he asked, putting down the darts.

"Seriously?" McKinley eyed him quizzically.

"Why not?" He extended his hand.

McKinley placed her hand in his and followed him onto the dance floor. As their bodies became one, the twinkling lights around the room seemed to only shine on them. Hand in hand and chest to chest, they slow danced to "Lovesong" by British sensation Adele. The strum from the guitar transported

McKinley and Koran to another realm in time.

No one else but them existed. To be in each other's arms felt right. It was like they belonged with one another. Koran rested his cheek on top of McKinley's head. Never in life did he think he'd ever feel this way again. Whitney had been the only woman for him. He never imagined he'd find someone who'd capture his heart the way she did.

McKinley, however, made him want to love again, being with her made him feel whole again. Her smile made him smile. For her, he'd put her hurt on his shoulders. Koran dreaded the fact that their journey was about to end. He wanted to stay with her forever.

McKinley pressed her face against Koran's chest, feeling the exact same way. For the last three years she'd had it all wrong. This was what love was supposed to feel like. It was uncomplicated and magical. A real man didn't put you in harm's way. He shielded you from pain. McKinley felt like she was floating on air.

She hadn't laughed and smiled this much in years. Koran brought out the best in her. She wanted to fix everything broken in him. He'd rescued her and she wanted to do the same. Koran placed his index finger underneath McKinley's chin and lifted her head up. She gazed up at him with tears in her eyes. After so much negativity, she'd found solace in something good.

Koran examined her face when suddenly a tear fell from her

eyes and landed on his heart. After that, he knew he couldn't be without her. McKinley stood on her tiptoes and kissed his lips. The bond they'd created was unbreakable. Some would even say bulletproof, but like all good things in life, what they shared had to come to an end.

XoXo

The rapid speed and constant rattling from the train jolted McKinley from side to side. For hours she'd tried to fall asleep, but the thoughts that raced through her head kept her awake. The closer she and Koran got to St. Louis, the more her mind filled with thoughts of dread. Over the last few days, the unexpected had happened.

She hadn't seen it coming, but it felt right. She'd fallen in love. With Koran, everything was different, but in a good way. From the day they'd met, he'd shown her more than Jamil had in the three years they'd been together. He made her feel like she mattered. He was generous and kind. He never left her out in the cold and, most importantly, his word was his bond. When he said he was going to do something, he did it, unlike Jamil.

Koran laughed at her sarcasm and silliness. He didn't put her down or bail every time she did something he didn't like or agree with. When she was down, he did whatever he could to lift her spirits. McKinley gazed over at him. Koran's head dangled to the side. He was asleep and snoring lightly. McKinley wanted to snuggle against him, but she didn't want to bother him.

Suddenly, Koran's eyes fluttered open and he looked over at her. McKinley grinned. She was slightly embarrassed that he'd caught her staring at him while he was asleep. She prayed to God he didn't think she was a creep.

"What you lookin' at, lil' lady?" He yawned.

"Nothin'," she lied.

"Come here." Koran wrapped his arm around her neck and pulled her close.

McKinley loved being in his embrace. She felt safe. Nothing else in the world mattered. If she could, she would've stayed in his arms forever. The sad part was that McKinley knew forever didn't exist for them. When they got to St. Louis, she'd have to confess to Koran that the last few days they'd shared were all they had. It would hurt like hell, but it was something she had to do.

McKinley wasn't mentally, financially or spiritually ready to be with him yet. She had to get her life on track and come to grips with everything that had happened between her and Jamil before she could even think about being with another man. Her mind was too bogged down with all of the lies Jamil told and trying to decipher what was real between her and Jamil and what was fake.

She didn't have a job, let alone a dime to her name, and her soul was too wounded to trust any man. At that moment and stage in her life, McKinley had to give herself over to God first before she could think of jumping into another relationship. She just prayed that once she was in a place of stability, Koran would still be open and available to lend her his heart.

Finally, after days of mayhem and pure madness, McKinley and Koran made it to St. Louis. Both couldn't have been happier. They'd finally get to see their loved ones' faces. Outside, in front of the train station, McKinley nervously teetered from one foot to another. She could barely breathe. At any second, Koran's cab or her mother would be arriving and she hadn't uttered a word to Koran about what she was feeling. Her mind knew that breaking things off with him before things got too deep was the best thing to do, but the notion made her feel like her chest was caving in.

"I know that look on your face," Koran interrupted her thoughts.

"Huh?" McKinley blinked.

"You haven't been yourself since we left Tennessee. What's on your mind?"

McKinley swallowed the huge lump in her throat and willed herself not to cry.

"What's wrong? Talk to me." Koran reached out for her hand.

"It's just that I really like you."

"I like you, too." He brushed her hair from out of her face. "So what's the problem?"

McKinley looked up to the sky as tears stung the brim of her eyes.

"The problem is that I wanna continue seeing you, but I can't be with anybody right now. I just got out of a three-year relationship that was built on a lie and insecurity, and what do I have to show for it? Nothing. I put all of me in a man and in the end, not only did he shit on me, but I lessened myself just to be with him. I put my whole entire life in that man's hands and look at me. I'm twenty-five years old and moving back in with my mama. I have to do things differently this time. And that means taking care of *me* before I can give myself to you."

"I ain't gon' front, I wish things could be different. My feelings are hurt, but I understand. But when you're ready, get at me." He reached for her phone and put his number in it.

McKinley knew that she should say something, but couldn't figure out the right words to express how she felt. It didn't help matters either that Koran's cab had arrived; therefore, official- ly putting an end to their cross-country affair.

"My cab is here. I guess I'll see you next lifetime."

"Bye." McKinley stepped forward and gave him a hug.

"Bye, McKinley." Koran hugged her back and kissed her on the cheek. "Don't make me wait too long." Koran reluctantly pulled away from her and picked up his bags.

McKinley stood back and watched with sadness in her eyes as Koran put his things in the trunk of the cab. Before hopping into the cab, Koran paused and looked at McKinley one last time. McKinley gazed back at him and forced a smile onto her face. Koran gave her a slight smile back and winked his eye. Seconds later, the cab pulled away from the curb and just like in the movies, McKinley stood on the sidewalk and watched until the cab disappeared into the sunset.

XoXo

"McKinley!" Kristen yelled from her car, waving her hand.

McKinley scanned the pick-up area at Miami International Airport until she spotted her friend. The two women locked eyes with one another and smiled. They hadn't seen each other in six months. McKinley happily walked across the parking lot with her suitcase in tow.

"Girl, look at you," Kristen exclaimed, getting out of the car. "You look so pretty."

McKinley's hair was filled with an abundance of spiral curls. She was dressed weather-appropriate in a grey sweatshirt, black mini-skirt and black combat boots.

"Thank you, so do you." McKinley hugged her friend tight.

"Girl, we got so much to catch up on," Kristen said, helping her place her bag in the trunk of the car. "You know me and

Tony broke up, right?"

"Yeah, you told me that about a month ago." McKinley got into the car.

"Well, now I'm seeing this guy named Rico and girl, he is so muthafuckin' sexy."

McKinley gazed out of the front windshield, trying her best to stay interested in Kristen's conversation, but where they were heading had her on edge. McKinley was going to visit Jamil's grave. Yes, she'd gotten her life together by going to school for an associate's degree in fashion merchandising, holding down a job as a salesperson for a boutique, purchasing her first car and renting a cozy one-bedroom studio apartment, but she and Jamil still had unfinished business.

McKinley thought that by accomplishing her goals she would feel better and be able to move on with her life peacefully. But all of the anger and pain she had for Jamil still resided deep within her heart. After months of analyzing why she still felt that way, she finally realized that she'd never gotten a chance to properly say good-bye.

She hadn't been able to attend the wake or the funeral because of the circumstances she'd been under. McKinley had been forced to move on without having any kind of closure. So here she was, back in Miami, praying to God that this experience would release all of the demons that haunted her day after day.

"We're here." Kristen pulled up to the curb.

McKinley looked around at the acres of grass and tombstones, remorsefully.

"His grave is right over there." Kristen pointed to her right. She put the car in park. "You need me to go wit' you?"

"No. I need to do this on my own." McKinley inhaled deeply, then got out.

Each footstep she took felt as if she was walking on grass made of quicksand. For a second, she wondered if she had made the wrong decision. Maybe visiting Jamil would do her more harm than good. She was already having shortness of breath. Her palms were sweaty and her vision was blurred. But she had to get the feelings she harbored off of her chest.

McKinley stood in front of Jamil's grave. His name, birth date and death date caused her whole entire body to shake. McKinley could even feel her eyelashes shaking. Swallowing hard, she allowed the tears that had been stinging her eyes to fall gracefully down her rosy cheeks.

"I thought that when I got here I'd know exactly what I wanted to say to you. But being here with you only makes me feel more confused. You know, for the last six months I've been trying to figure out the point of our relationship. I've tried so hard to figure out why for three years you made me believe that you loved me and that we had a future.

"I thought about it when I woke up, when I brushed my

teeth, when I pee'd, when I sat in traffic, when I ate dinner alone. I thought about it so much that it made my head hurt. But you know what I realized?" She pulled out a tissue from her purse and wiped her nose.

"I realized that like everything else in your life, I was just another game that you loved to play. You knew how I felt about you. You knew that I loved you and that I would do anything for you. You knew that I would never leave you and that's why you did every fucked-up thing under the sun to me." McKinley became angry.

"I let you get away with so much for so long that the shit you did became a big-ass joke to you. I should've known you weren't shit when you cheated on me twice, when you stood me up fifty-million times, when you gave me the silent treatment when you were the one who was wrong." She sniffled.

"I should've walked away from yo' ass then, but like a dummy I stayed 'cause I thought you would eventually change. I believed you every single time you sat in my face and told me that you wouldn't hurt me anymore. Every time you promised me you'd do better, I prayed to God and I said, 'God, please let this time be different'." McKinley looked up at the sky and let her tears fall out of the corners of her eyes.

"And every time," she looked back down at his headstone, "you made me out to look like a complete and utter idiot. You hurt me so much that it got to the point where I'd rather put up wit' your shit than be alone. My love for you became more important than my self-worth. I knew in my head that the way you treated me wasn't right, but I wanted to be with you and be in a relationship so bad that I made myself believe that the things you did to me were okay." She cried uncontrollably.

"I forgot that real love doesn't hurt all the time. Yeah, in a relationship you have problems, but we had a problem every other day. *Every* day." She stressed the word every. "When I woke up every morning, I'd wonder: *What's going to happen today?* With you I had to always be on guard 'cause I never knew what you were going to do next. Then, after I thought you'd done everything humanly possible to hurt me, you go and die on me. And I thought that was the worse, but then you sucker-punched me again." She threw up her hands then slapped them down onto her thighs.

"I learned that not only were you married with kids, but that you had a whole 'nother girlfriend and kids. Hell, I wasn't even your mistress. I was your number two girlfriend. So I guess you never had any intention on marrying me. You only proposed to me to keep me content a little while longer." She broke down and cried even harder.

After a short pause, McKinley wiped her eyes and inhaled deeply.

"I swear to God I wanna hate you so bad, but I can't." She shook her head.

"I'm just mad as hell at myself for letting things go on so long. But I'm here today, Jamil, to tell you that despite everything you've done to me. I still love you, but I'm letting you go." McKinley took her engagement ring out of her purse.

"There will be no more wondering and guessing what your intentions were 'cause it was what it was. You were a liar and you didn't mean me any good and that's all I need to know now." She placed the ring on top of his headstone, caught up in the moment.

Before walking away, McKinley took one last look at Jamil's grave. This would be the first and last time she'd ever visit him. It was now time for her to put the past behind her and move on to the good part of her life that God had in store for her. As she walked toward Kristen's car, McKinley quickly came to her senses and ran back over to Jamil's grave and picked up the ring.

"I may be dumb, but I ain't stupid. I can put this muthafucka on eBay."

XOXO

After visiting Jamil's grave, life for McKinley got even easier. It was as if a weight had been lifted off of her shoulders. She was able to breathe again without feeling like she was going to be sick. Sleepless nights no longer existed. She was finally at a place of peace. But there was one thing she had left to do.

McKinley stood on the balcony of her apartment. The sun was out in full view. Birds were chirping and the leaves from the trees swayed in the wind. With her phone in her hand, McKinley said a silent prayer to God. *God, please don't let him have forgotten about me.* She dialed Koran's number. For the last six months she hadn't been able to get him out of her mind. She missed him dearly and couldn't wait to hear the sound of his voice again.

"Hello?" he answered in a low and raspy tone.

"Hi," McKinley uttered softly.

Koran held the phone close to his ear and smiled. He'd been waiting for this day for months.

"It took you long enough," he finally said.

"I know." McKinley laughed. "I miss you."

"I miss you, too. So when can I come see you?" Koran asked.

"The sooner, the better."

Part Four

"*Let' keep it G, nobody se you when you being humble.*"

Wale

"Chain Music"

O sat in his souped up Bentley Mulsanne. The windows were tinted, with peanut butter interior and leather seats with the Louis Vuitton symbol covering every inch: the leather, roof, even on his steering wheel, and O loved showing it off.

O was scrolling through his Instagram feed and felt disgusted looking at some of the fraudulent things that niggas took pictures of, trying to stunt. It made him think back on his own days as a runner for Koran, before he became his own boss.

O used to walk around, draped in diamond chains with diamonds that weren't even close to the clarity that he had now. He felt like he looked like a clown then, rather than the legend he looks like now. All the niggas knew who he was, and what he had to offer, and he was proud of his success.

A few years ago, he was Koran's loyal worker. He never did anything too bad to get on Koran's bad side, or so he thought. All O wanted to do was to get money and shine on niggas. Growing up, he was teased for not having a lot of money for clothes, shoes, hell, his momma didn't even have enough money to buy lotion. The kids in school used to make fun of him and call him ashy. It broke his heart. The only person who was nice to him was Trina. They grew up around the way from each other, and whenever someone tried to get on him, she always stood up for him.

He always promised that he would protect her, and he

thought he was doing that when he introduced her to Koran. But all that nigga ever did was lie to her, and he hit her a few times. On top of that, Koran had the audacity to beat him within an inch of his life at the club, just because he thought he was flirting with his little slut-dead-ho.

O still held a grudge on that, and was biding his time. He might have been impatient with getting money and bitches, but there was nothing that would allow him to rush a good revenge scheme. But before that could happen, he was in the same position that Koran had been in many times with him. Waiting outside of the police station, waiting for one of his soldiers to come out.

While waiting, O took out his cell phone and took a picture of his watch, and then a selfie of himself in his car. He uploaded the pictures on Instagram, with the captions: "Money talks, so I don't have to. #geechi."

Almost immediately he started getting likes, and responses. As he was looking at who all from his twelve thousand friends were liking his photos, someone knocked on his window. He looked up and saw his soldier Beans, who just got released.

"Hey, dude, I'm sorry, bruh, they gave me all this bullshit paperwork to fill out," Beans said, sliding into the passenger seat.

O shrugged his shoulders at Beans. He didn't appreciate him making him wait, but he needed Beans and his new connect. Otherwise, he would have made him disposable right then and there. Beans continued to make excuses for his behavior, but O zoned out while he was talking. He didn't feel like listening to Beans as he explained why this fuck up was different from all of the others.

Beans, whose day job was at a jewelry store that O set up for him, was to not show people jewelry until they put down a non-refundable deposit to look at the jewelry. Then he was supposed to split that money with O. But, Beans got too rude and a customer complained about Beans. He was arrested for stealing, but thanks to O, after he handled the store owner, he won't be pressing charges. However, Beans is now going to be watched by the police after all of this, and that can only mean that they'll be watching O, too. So, he needed to get Beans' connect, and then separate himself from him.

"Just tell me about your new connect," O said, cutting Beans off.

Beans looked a little baffled that O would just stop him from talking, but then decided to just go for it. "Yeah, it's this girl I knew back from Dade County. She was big there, sold yayo, h, m, ex, and any other letter you can think of," Beans joked. He turned to O to see if he caught his joke, but O just stared ahead while he drove.

"But why is she coming here? Why don't she just stay in Florida?"

"She said that she's looking to expand. She used to spend some time here, and she said she has some unfinished business to take care of here. So her expansion could help her complete whatever goal she needed."

At a stop light, O picked up his phone and went into his contacts. He scrolled down until he came to the name "Junior" on his phone. O turned to Beans, "Hey, I need to make a phone call real quick."

"Cool, man." Beans nodded and looked out the passenger window. He knew that O was mad at him, but he was one of his biggest sellers, and even though he fucked up this time, he knew he could get things back in line for O. On top of that, this expansion deal he was telling O about would bring in big paper for O and him. He couldn't even calculate what the finder's fee was gonna be on this.

"Hey man, I'm down the block... Alright, I'll see you soon." O turned back to Beans. "Sorry, I had to tell Junior I was on my way. He's waiting on me." O turned his attention back to the road and began driving once the light turned green. "So what's the girl's name?"

"Well, she's had to change her name a few times to keep from being caught, but right now I think she goes by Ashley."

O nodded his head. "Alright, do you have Ashley's number?" he asked as he pulled up to one of his trap houses' driveway and pushed the remote to make the garage door slowly rise.

Beans nodded his head, while the car slowly entered the garage. "Yeah, you want me to give it to you?" Three men came into the garage, as the garage door slowly made its descent, enclosing the car.

"Just give me your phone."

Beans looked at O surprised. "Uh, alright." The moment that Beans handed O his phone, the passenger door flew open. The three big men pulled Beans out in a quick, swift motion. One immediately covered his mouth, and the three men dragged him out of the car while he was kicking and trying to scream for help.

The terrified look on Beans' face would have affected anyone else, but O. O looked at Beans, disgusted that this nigga was fine getting caught while doing his job. O's been to jail many of times, but it was always on unrelated incidents, like parking violations, or disturbing the peace. Nothing that shone a light on his dark dealings. But Beans stealing was going to be too much of a light on what they did, and O couldn't have that. So, he would take Ashley's information, dispose of Beans phone, and then continue to get this money without him.

His boys knew what he wanted to do, and he knew that Beans' body wouldn't be found. When the men finally got Beans' thrashing body into the house, O opened the garage door and reversed down the driveway. As the garage door lowered, Beans' muffled pleas were heard over his car engine.

That was the problem with luxury cars, their engines always purred. But a good thing was that they had bomb stereo set ups. O turned on the radio and blasted ASAP Rocky's "Fuckin' Problems" as he drove away.

XoXo

Trina examined her toned body in the mirror as she just got out of the shower. She reveled in the feel of the hot water washing away the sweat and toxins that resulted from her working out, and as she dried off, she felt very accomplished. While most women were too busy sleeping and eating, she was working on her body, her most prized possession.

As the sound of the gardener's lawnmower, cutting her acre of lawn invaded her thoughts, Trina smiled at her naked form. On her side of the his and hers double vanity, she grabbed her Shiseido facial moisturizer and smoothed it all over her face, neck, and décolletage. She then grabbed her L'Occitane Ultra-Rich body cream and began to smother that on her body. As she bent down and worked it up from her ankles to her stomach, she felt sexy. Her body was smooth and tight, and since she'd been waist training, her hips and butt poked out more, and gave her already crazy body a more precise visual of an hour glass shape.

As she worked the cream over her breast, she caught a glimpse of herself in the mirror and smiled. Yes, she was a bad bitch, and she wasn't ashamed to admit that. Her body looked better than not only the women of her own age, but even better than some of the teens in her son's school. Women were letting themselves slip all over the place, and she refused to be one of them.

Trina's body got her everything that she ever wanted in life. From the moment she began to develop, she knew the power that her body held over men and she worked it to her advantage. She was Kim Kardashian before Kim Kardashian, and she was proud.

Men followed her and begged to not just be in her presence, but to shower her with gifts, and she encouraged them, until she met Koran. He was her first true love. She thought that Brandon, her son Malik's father was, but after he did her dirty and left her after giving birth to Malik, Koran taught her what true love was. He wasn't just faithful to her, but he loved her throughout all of her faults, and put up with her whenever she was too much. But she did things for him, too. She supported him while he owned the streets of St. Louis, and she was his queen. But, she made a huge mistake when she cheated on him with a guy who wasn't even that important. Trina didn't want to, it was the attention. She was addicted to it, and anytime that it seemed like a man wanted to treat her to gifts or for some face time, she didn't mind obliging, but it cost her everything at the time that she needed Koran the most.

Koran helped to raise her son, Malik, ever since he was four years old. He didn't have to be obligated to him, but he was, and made sure that Malik never went without. But it was hard for her to know that Koran was only in her son's life, instead of hers, so she did whatever she could to get him back, but when Koran re-connected up with Whitney, she knew she lost him forever.

Trina walked over to her personal walk in closet. On the right of the door frame were all of her dresses. In front of her were all of her shoes, rows and rows of shoes. To the left were her shirts, blouses, and her pants. She grabbed a pair of red Lanvin sweat pants, and threw on a black Chloe crop top, with matching red and black Prada leather high tops to complete the look.

She went back to the mirror and pushed her hair up in a top knot and secured it with bobbin pins.

After her life with Koran, Trina never thought that she would love anyone again, and she just went on from one big named drug dealer, to the next. Until a chance meeting at a boutique, when a man that she normally wasn't interested in stopped her. While shopping with the money her boyfriend gave her, a man named Marcus stopped her and asked her for advice on what to get his mother. Marcus didn't look bad. He was a clean cut, dark skinned man with a very muscular build to him, but he looked at least ten years older than her and seemed too boring for her. She was used to being involved with drug dealers, not someone so safe.

Marcus was a top level executive at an insurance firm. After about twenty minutes of him asking her annoying questions about things that she liked, he finally let her know that he wasn't interested in what to get his mother, he was interested in her, and he asked her out. She turned him down, but he gave her his number. As they both left, and she saw him get in his Mercedes S class, she decided to give him a chance, and it ended up working out. They fell in love and got married a year ago.

Marcus promised her that he would always look out for her, and give her everything she ever desired, and he did. Marcus did his best to meet all of her needs, financially and emotionally, but Trina was sad to admit that she still felt empty. Even though she lived in a five bedroom, four bathroom mansion, that boasted twenty foot high vaulted ceilings in the great room in the elite Ladue neighborhood, she still wanted something that Marcus couldn't give her, and it was excitement. The truth was, Trina was addicted to dysfunction, and though the life that she set up with Marcus was safe, it was boring to her. It was as if she needed drama to survive, as much as she needed oxygen.

After applying some Dior eye shadow and a bright red lip, she looked in the mirror and still felt empty, like a beautiful

Faberge Egg, exquisitely decorated, but completely hollow inside. She walked over to a container on her vanity and opened it. Inside it was filled with Q-tips. As she dug inside, she pulled out a small baggie of cocaine, a mirror, and a razor in a protective cover.

After she placed the small mirror on the vanity, she dropped a small amount of cocaine on the mirror, and chopped it up with her razor into two straight lines. She grabbed a receipt that was left on the vanity, rolled it up, and then began to quickly inhale the first line of coke off of the mirror. As she rose, she looked at herself in the mirror again, and wiped off the residue from her nose.

She left her en suite and went into the bedroom, where she had a clear view of the back yard. Devin, their White gardener was on a riding lawnmower, finishing the backyard. Trina descended the stairs, and walked to the back door with intense focus. She stood at the backdoor, watching the sun reflect off of Devin's ivory skin. It was autumn, and Devin was wearing a black long sleeve shirt, but he had his sleeves rolled up. The wind blew through the thick puffs of dark brown hair that stuck out from under his Cardinals baseball cap.

After a few minutes, Devin could feel Trina's intense stare and looked in her direction. A smile spread across his face, Trina smiled back.

Once he got done, he jumped down from the lawnmower

and approached her. The two stood in the house's back doorway, where the sexual tension was palpable. Trina had poured him a glass of water and handed it to him.

"Hi Mrs. Williams, how are you today?" Devin's gaze was intense, compared to Trina's that had now grown glossy, due to the drugs.

"I'm great, how are you?" Trina arched her back toward him as he drank down the cup of water in two gulps, emphasizing her curves.

"I'm doing great." Devin placed the glass on the nearest counter top and then removed his cap and ruffled his hair to remove the imprint that the hat left on his tresses.

Trina's fingers tingled with the anticipation of not just running her hands through his hair, but tugging on it while he thrust between her legs. "My husband told me that he paid you this week, but I wanted to give you a tip, do you mind coming upstairs so I can get my purse?"

"Of course." Devin's penis immediately grew from arousal. The two had been sleeping together for the last two months, and Devin was beginning to become addicted to Trina's body. He dreamt about the way that her hips swirled when she rode him, and how her tongue expertly glided up and down his shaft when she gave him head.

Once they reached Trina and Marcus's bedroom, Trina walked over to her purse and pulled out a condom. "Is this payment okay?"

Devin walked closer to her, they both inhaled each other's scents and pheromones. Devin reached down to Trina's chin with his hand and lifted her face to meet his, and then he lowered his lips to hers.

Trina felt like she was drowning in his passion, his lust, and most importantly, the drama that went along with being with him. He pushed Trina to a sitting position on the bed. She looked up at him seductively as she unbuttoned his pants and slowly pulled down the zipper. His stiff erection caused the material in his boxers to rise. Trina pulled down Devin's jeans and boxers at the same time, and was then met with his long, pink member.

Trina didn't know if she loved him, but she knew that she loved the feeling of excitement that he gave her; a sense of control in an environment that she felt she had little control over. This wasn't her house, though her name was on the deed. It wasn't her money that she spent, it was the money that her husband gave her. But this was *her* body and she could make anyone that she wanted feel special with it.

Instinctually she brought his tip to her mouth and slowly licked around the head like it was a lollipop. Devin groaned with desire as Trina worked her mouth around the head. He placed his hand on her top knot as she moved her head back and forth along the shaft of his penis. As one hand followed her mouth, the other began to gently fondle his testicles and his groans got louder. Trina could feel his veins throbbing, and she moved faster, wanting to make him cum, until he stopped her.

"Wait," he stepped away from her. He stepped out of his pants and boxers. "I need to thank you for my bonus." He bent down and removed her shoes and placed them to the right of him, and then he slowly pulled off her pants. He was surprised when he realized that she hadn't put on any underwear. He could tell she had been waiting for him. He gently pushed her to lie back on the bed. Trina scooted back to allow him some room on the mattress as he removed his shirt and then settled down on the bed between Trina's legs.

Devin gazed longingly at her clit and placed her legs on his shoulders. He led a trail of kisses to her vagina, and right before he got there, he started kissing the inside of her other thigh. Trina arched her back in anticipation and removed her shirt and bra. She began massaging her breasts, and squeezing her nipples.

Devin loved seeing Trina play with herself, and his lust led him to dive head first into her vagina. As his tongue maneuvered its way around her clit, Trina slowly grinded her hips in the direction that his tongue was. Devin couldn't pry his eyes away from Trina as she moaned in pleasure while pinching and twisting her nipples tighter as Devin switched from licking to sucking her clit. It began to grow in arousal, and Devin's penis began to drip from his excitement for giving her pleasure.

Once he realized that he couldn't contain himself anymore, he stood up, placed the condom on, and then climbed on top of Trina. With one easy motion, he entered her and their bodies began to move in unison. She wrapped her arms around his back that was muscular from all of the yard work that he completed as a living.

As her feet began to tingle, and a warm sensation moved up her feet to up her stomach, she knew that this was the life for her. A husband who would give her the world, and a boyfriend that would meet all of her excitement needs. She needed the drama in her life, and as she came, while Devin still proceeded to stroke inside of her, prolonging his own orgasm until she was done, she knew that she should've felt bad for how she wanted to live her life. But she didn't.

"*I feel like you were made just for me, babe.*"

Musiq Soulchild

"*So Beautiful*"

Professor Lewis was standing in front of the lecture hall of about 40 students. The professor's notes were displayed on a large screen behind him. He moved the cursor to highlight important points of the text, before clicking to make the slideshow go to a new page. McKinley was taking notes in her Merchandising course when her phone's loud alert sounded in the middle of the lecture. McKinley's face turned red as she fumbled into her purse to look for her phone. A few students glanced toward her, and the professor continued to lecture, though he wore a noticeable annoyed look on his face as he continued.

McKinley grabbed her phone and saw that she had received a text message.

From: Koran

SEX! Now that I have ur attention what time u gonna meet me?

Sent: Friday, September 19

McKinley burst out laughing. She didn't realize how loud she was until more people turned to look at her and the professor glared at her even more.

"I'm sorry," McKinley began to gather her belongings. "I'll just take this outside."

"Please do," Professor Lewis said while rolling his eyes. He sighed and then went back to his notes.

McKinley knew that she probably should have stayed to hear the professor break down his notes, but she knew that they were also online, so she could catch up after her date with Koran tonight.

McKinley grabbed her phone and dialed him once she got out of the building. As the phone rang she sat on a bench just outside of the building. A breeze blew past her, causing her loose curls to waft in the wind. As the wind died down, her hair fell back on her shoulders. McKinley adjusted her aqua colored off-the-shoulder Jamison sweater. She shifted her butt on the hard bench and crossed her feet at the ankles where her Betsey Johnson black wedge sneakers met.

"Hello," Koran answered, laughing and swiveling in his office chair.

"Hi, asshole!" McKinley greeted him, laughing. "I can't believe you texted me that! I had to leave class 'cause I couldn't stop laughing."

"Sorry, let me make it up to you."

"Oh yeah, you're making it up to me, alright," McKinley said, watching other students walk past her. "What do you want to do tonight?"

Koran continuously twisted a pen between his index and middle fingers. "Well, I was thinking that maybe I could pick you up and we can start out the night at the art museum?"

McKinley smiled. After all of the bullshit that Jamil put her through, it was nice to have a man in her life that made plans that he stuck with. She'd been dating Koran for a few months and things were already exponentially better than they were within the three years she was with Jamil. "You know something, even though I grew up here, I've never been to the art museum before."

"What? You're gonna love it. Harlow and I always go whenever there's a new exhibit."

McKinley felt a twinge of uneasiness when Koran mentioned his daughter. She felt horrible to admit it to herself, but she'd never been in a situation where she had to compete for another man's affection. She thought that Harlow was an adorable child, but McKinley was scared. She didn't spend a lot of time with kids, and she didn't even think she really liked kids all that much. But she knew that she really liked Koran, and if being with him meant being with his daughter, she would at least try.

"Am I spending the night?" McKinley asked, hopeful. Even though she knew that Koran really liked her, he was still very protective of Harlow, and didn't want to just thrust other people in her life yet.

"Not tonight, but I do have an idea though." Koran didn't let McKinley know, but he could sense McKinley's hesitation with his daughter, and he had to let her know that they were a package deal. He couldn't be in her life unless his daughter was there also. "Tomorrow is my guy, Malik's—"

McKinley brushed some dirt off of her jeans, "the kid that you helped raise, right?"

Koran smiled. He liked the fact that McKinley really listened to him. Most of the women he tried dating only waited for their turn to speak. Whitney was the only other person to actively listen to him and that meant a lot. "Well, he's not so much a kid anymore. It's his 15th birthday, and each year I take him out to eat. Harlow's normal nanny is actually going out of town, and I didn't want to bring Harlow with us. Do you think you could watch her for me? It'll give you a chance to really get to know her one on one."

McKinley immediately felt a sense of worry, but she reminded herself that this is what she must do to be with Koran. "Of course, do I need to bring anything?" McKinley didn't know what children were involved with, or how to entertain them.

"Nah, she's pretty low maintenance. Just bring you, she has toys. You'll just have to spend a little time wit' her. Send her off to play wit' her toys if she gets to be too much, and then you two can eat lunch. I have some frozen pizzas in the fridge. You can just heat one of those up. You think you can do this?"

The school's bell rang, and McKinley stood up and started walking to her car slowly with her messenger bag slung across her shoulder. "Of course I can. Anything for you."

"Alright, baby, I'll pick you up at 5:30."

"See you then, baby," McKinley smiled and disconnected the phone call. McKinley was excited, but had a small sense of worry when it came to tomorrow's babysitting date with Harlow.

XoXo

The setting sun reflected an orange glow on the practice helmets for Ladue Horton Watkins High School's football team. There was a sea of white helmets as the players' heads were down, ready for the play to start. Malik's mind raced on other pressing matters as Ed Hill, the quarterback, yelled the play that they were going to run. At the snap of the ball, Malik looked up, and began to run to receive the ball. As the ball came flying at him, he missed it. A sharp whistle invaded his thoughts as he was internally yelling at himself. As if his coach was reading his mind, and realizing that Malik wasn't being hard enough on himself, he filled in.

"What the hell was that, Malik?" The coach yelled in his face.

"I was--"

"I don't care what excuses you have, you didn't catch the fuckin' ball!" The coach threw his clip board on the ground. The coach ripped his whistle off of his neck and threw it at Malik's chest.

"What's the point of you being a wide receiver if you're not receiving the fucking ball?"

Malik stood there silently, looking down at the field while all eyes were on him. Everyone seemed to be expecting a reaction, but Malik didn't deliver.

"Just get the fuck out of here! Come back when you remember what the fuck you were supposed to do, and how to do it!"

Malik finally looked up at his coach's eyes, and glared at him. Malik wanted to yell back, but Koran always taught him to respect authority, no matter what. Plus, Malik knew that the only reason why the coach was so angry was due to the fact that he was fucking up. He wasn't paying attention to what he was supposed to do, and he was allowing all of the issues from his personal life to weigh him down.

Malik took off his helmet and walked off the field to the locker room to shower and change. As he walked, he didn't notice the black Escalade, fitted with chrome rims across the street, and the individual who was watching him.

Malik was walking home when the Escalade began to keep pace with him. Malik was so lost in his thoughts that he didn't realize the driver's side window rolled down.

"Hey lil' nigga."

Malik jumped and then immediately regretted it. If there was one thing that he learned in life, it was to never show any type of vulnerability, because the moment you did, that's when people take advantage of you. Most of people in Malik's life were vultures, just posted up, looking, waiting, hoping to get a scent of the possibility of decay, so they could gleefully watch other people's destruction and then enjoy themselves in the spoils of someone else's demise.

Malik looked into the car and saw O. *This nigga*, Malik thought in his head and kept on walking.

O kept the car in pace with Malik. "So you just not gonna say anything back, lil nigga?"

Malik wasn't in the mood for dealing with O's shit today. He had too much on his plate, but he also knew how persistent O was, and that he would continue to follow him to the ends of the Earth until he got the respect that he felt everyone should bestow upon him.

Malik rolled his eyes. "What's up, dude?"

"I should be asking you that. You seemed to have had a bad day at practice. What's up with you?"

Malik stopped walking and stared at O. "You were watching me?"

"Yeah," O said matter-of-factly, completely disregarding how creeped out Malik appeared to be.

Malik slightly shook his head and went back walking.

"Look, yo' momma wanted me to keep an eye out on you, and I promised her that I would. But, also, I have something that I wanted to talk to you about. Get in the car."

Malik kept on walking, looking straight ahead. "Nah, I'm good."

"Lil' nigga, that wasn't a suggestion." Malik stopped again and looked at O as he stopped his car alongside Malik. O's eyes were intense, and even though Malik didn't feel like being bothered, he didn't like dealing with O whenever he had that crazy look in his eyes. "Now get in the fuckin' car."

Malik looked around, and didn't really see anyone else. *No witnesses, damnit.* He then saw a car a block away with very tinted windows, and Malik knew it had to be someone in O's army. O always had someone locked and loaded trailing him, just in case someone wanted to jumped wild, or be disrespectful. Malik rolled his eyes and walked around to the passenger side and got in.

"What's up, dude?"

O started driving around the block. "Nothing much, homie. I got a proposition for you."

Malik immediately knew what O was about to say, and he'd turned him down already. He didn't know why O didn't get the hint. "Nah, I'm good on that."

"Lil' nigga, how are you good? You think that football playing is going to actually do something for you?"

"It's better than being posted up on the block all day."

O laughed and looked at Malik. "Why don't you ask Terrell Owens, or Ochocinco? Those niggas were two talented motherfuckers in the game, and now look at them. Don't have a pot to piss in or a window to throw it out of."

Malik looked out the window. He knew that O was telling the truth, but he promised Koran a long time ago that he would stay away from the block. After years of Koran trapping, he left the block and was able to open multiple businesses, and didn't have to worry about the police arresting him, or someone shooting at him. Malik knew that the money he could make trapping would be great, and most boys started at this age anyway. He could move out of his mother's and stepfather's house the moment he graduated high school, but he didn't want to go down that road. It usually led to either death or prison, and neither one looked appealing to Malik. Especially after what Vanessa shared with him a month ago.

"I'm offering you a chance to be able to make some real paper. Not that measly shit that Koran chucks at you for sweeping his stores."

"I told you, O, I'm good. I don't need anything extra."

"But what about your momma? You just gonna leave her high and dry like that?" O circled the block that Malik lived on while they still talked.

"What do you mean? My momma don't want for nothing." Malik looked around and saw that the tinted car was parked across the street from his house. Though he couldn't see who was watching him, he knew that whoever was in the car had their eyes firmly placed on O's car.

"*Now*. She's fine now, but she will need you to be the man around the house one day. Yo momma's been doing whatever she could to make sure that she kept a roof over your head, even after Koran up and almost left y'all stranded. Now you telling me that you wouldn't do anything to make sure that she's good? That's the least you could do." O stopped in front of Malik's house and Malik opened the door. "Just think about it, lil nigga. I know that you have a little girlfriend, too. I know she needs some extra dough as well."

Malik hid his disgust for O as he looked back at him. If he wasn't one hundred percent sure that the extra car was O's muscle, then Malik would have swung on O, just on principle alone. However, he knew that swinging on the leader of a drug cartel would have him either hurt or killed, so he left it alone. "I'll think about it."

"A'ight, stay up, lil' nigga." O pulled out of Malik's parents' driveway. Malik watched O and the car that was following him drive away before he went into the house.

"Hello?" Malik yelled into the house. He knew that his mother was probably out shopping. That seemed like the only thing she did these days. Shop and work out, always needing to be the finest woman in whatever room she was in.

Right then, Malik's cell phone rang. Not really looking at

the screen, he pressed the phone button and answered the call.

"Hello?" A feminine voice filled Malik's ears and a smile immediately spread across his face. Vanessa's voice always made him happy. No matter what kind of trash had happened to him, Vanessa always knew how to brighten up his day.

Vanessa and Malik met their freshman year of high school and had been dating ever since. When his grades began to drop in science and he was threatened with being dropped from football, she was his student tutor. Because he didn't want to seem stupid around her, he made sure to pay attention and raised his grade two whole letter grades in a matter of months.

The moment he saw her, he knew he wanted to be with her. All the students were required to wear a school uniform, but Vanessa always accessorized hers in a way that made it uniquely her. Her long, thick hair was almost like an accessory of its own. All hers, she always wore it in a new style that all the girls loved and envied at the same time. However, Vanessa couldn't care less what others thought about her. She always seemed like she was above the typical high school drama and if anyone tried to bring it to her, she could cut it down in less than two sentences. Vanessa did not play.

"What up, ma?"

"Hey," Vanessa's voice seemed to brighten as well when she heard Malik's. "I'm just leaving work. Wait... what are you doing home so early? I was calling to leave you an 'I love you' voicemail."

"Man, coach was being a dick. Kicked me out of practice."

"Alright, bye," Malik could hear Vanessa saying to her co-workers as she left.

Vanessa always knew that she wanted to work with kids, so when a position at a daycare opened up as an assistant, she jumped at the opportunity.

Vanessa's mind was always on the future, and she always tried to make sure that every step she made was a step in the right direction. She always knew that she wanted to go to a highly rated college, and she made sure that she put herself in a good academic position to do so. She also knew that she loved kids, and decided at a young age that she would open a chain of her own daycare facilities after she got a degree in business. She made sure that she was at the top of her class and did the tutoring extracurricular program during study hall to secure her place. However, recent issues caused her to up her participation, to ensure that she could get in and escape her home life.

"You hear me?" Malik said, annoyed. He hated when Vanessa ignored him on the phone.

Vanessa turned her attention back to the phone. "I'm sorry, baby. I'm just not used to talking to you at this time. Plus, I'm exhausted. But why did Coach Norwood kick you out of practice?"

Malik flopped down on the tan sectional sofa, and grabbed

the remote for the TV. "Because I wasn't paying attention… and he was right." Malik laid his head back and closed his eyes, trying to forget how he embarrassed himself at practice.

Vanessa immediately felt guilty. "I'm sorry, baby. You want me to come over?"

Malik lifted his head. "Yeah."

Vanessa smiled, "I'll be there in a few."

Malik smiled as the two disconnected their phones. He took his stuff out of the living room and the dining room and put his book bag and football equipment in his room when the doorbell rang. Malik ran down the stairs and walked over and looked through the peephole. He smiled when he saw Vanessa looking back at him.

He opened the door and Vanessa walked in.

"How are my babies doing?" Malik asked, kissing Vanessa and placing a hand on her stomach.

Vanessa laughed and passionately kissed Malik. After she pulled away, she smiled at him, "We're fine." His heart immediately melted. He knew he would do anything for her.

Vanessa and Malik were trying to be as safe as possible when they first started having sex, but they must have screwed up at some time, because Vanessa became pregnant. After talking about abortion for a few weeks, they decided to keep the baby, and Malik was determined to be a real father to him, or her, unlike the unknown deadbeat that was his father.

Vanessa smiled as Malik helped take her book bag off of her. She placed her hands on her lower back and she stretched, poking out her flat stomach. She was only about six weeks pregnant, so she wasn't showing yet. "We're just tired and hungry. Do you have anything that I can eat? I am starving!"

Malik walked into the kitchen, and Vanessa followed him. He went over to the cabinet, pulled out a large can of tuna, and grabbed the can opener from the counter. "I was just about to make tuna," Malik began, but then stopped himself when he noticed the nauseated look on Vanessa's face.

Vanessa thought she had hidden it, but apparently not well enough. "Sorry, baby, but just thinking about it is making me nauseous. Why don't we go somewhere and get something to eat?" Vanessa's eyes lit up, "Tacos would be amazing right now."

Malik sighed, "I wish. My Mama's been borrowing money from me a lot lately."

"She hasn't paid it back to you?" Vanessa looked confused.

"Nah, and I'm really confused about what she's spending it on. Marcus gives her all the money he can, but she keeps on using my money. I just don't understand it."

Vanessa rubbed her stomach, and looked guilty. Tears began to well up in her eyes. "I am so sorry, baby." Vanessa sat down at the kitchen table and buried her face in her hands.

Malik pulled the other seat next to her and sat down. He

rubbed her back, knowing that her fit of emotion was only due to being pregnant. Vanessa rarely cried about anything, she was too rational.

"Don't worry about it, baby. You know how my mama can get. She's just petty."

Vanessa began to rub the tears away from her eyes. Her eye make-up streaked her face. Malik knew that if she saw the runny makeup that it would make her cry even more, so he grabbed a paper napkin from the table and began to wipe her face.

"Thanks, baby," Vanessa sighed. "Look, why don't I drive, and I'll even pay? You had a rough day, you deserve for some-one to treat you as well as you treat me."

Malik recoiled in horror. "What type of nigga am I gonna look like having my girl pay for me? I got this." Malik ran up-stairs into his room and ransacked it until he found about ten dollars in some dirty jean's pockets.

They both walked out to Vanessa's car, a royal blue Ford Mustang coup. Malik never wanted to make Vanessa uncom-fortable, and he trusted her so much, but there were things that didn't add up to him. Vanessa's mother was a drug addict, and he couldn't understand how Vanessa was able to have such an extravagant car, but she told him that her father left her an inheritance that her mother didn't have access to. Whenever he asked her, her answer never changed, and she never showed herself to be anything less than trustworthy from the moment he met her.

They got in the car, and she turned to him. She could see that his mind was flooded with thoughts. She leaned over and gave him a kiss that brought him back to the present. He slowly pushed her back.

"Don't squish my baby," he smiled at her.

Vanessa laughed and then started the car. As they drove away, Malik didn't notice that O's car was parked two blocks away, and he kept his eyes glued to Vanessa's car as the two drove away.

O smirked as he watched the car disappear into the distance. He grabbed his cell phone out of his center console and dialed Ashley.

"Hello?" A woman's voice filled O's ears.

"Yeah, Beans told me that you wanted to meet me?" O was beaming from ear to ear.

"Yes, when do you want to meet?"

O looked at his diamond encrusted Rolex. "Are you free now?"

"Yeah, is Beans coming with you?"

O began to laugh, "Yeah, about that."

Part Five

"Could you just lie to me,
lie to me, lie to me so sweet?

Baby, ignorance is bliss,
yeah I know exactly
what this is."

Miguel

"Pussy is Mine"

McKinley and Koran left from having an amazing night. They started off at the Art Museum, where McKinley bought a print of a photograph that she saw, then they went to dinner at the restaurant Three Sixty.

Three Sixty was a beautifully decorated upscale restaurant in the heart of St. Louis. It was named Three Sixty because it gave an aerial view of the city. With rooftop seating, a customer could take in all of the breathtaking beauty that the city had to offer.

Koran made a reservation for a private booth on the East-side of the restaurant. It was perfect, they could people watch from their own private booth, without the noise of the excited patrons, and they could take in the beauty of the Arch, the Mississippi River, and the lights from downtown as they shone brightly.

The anticipation between the two was extremely palpable as Koran waited patiently as McKinley unlocked the front door of her apartment.

As he followed her in and she turned on the light, he admired the new touches that she seemed to add each time he came over. It was like McKinley was expressing herself with each decorative touch, and she was letting him see the real her. The more he got to know about McKinley, the more he felt like he was falling in love with her.

McKinley walked over to a closet and pulled out an empty

picture frame. She took the black and white sketch that she got from the Museum's gift shop, *In the Box*, and placed it in the frame.

The sketch was of a naked woman who was lying on the ground, with her body partially in a box. For some reason McKinley felt like she could relate to the sketch and she wanted to display it in her apartment.

Once the sketch was in a frame, McKinley held it out in front of her, and tried to figure out which wall to put it on.

As McKinley twisted her body, holding the framed picture, Koran couldn't stop himself from admiring her frame. *She is so sexy*. McKinley wore a purple Diane Von Furstenberg printed wrap dress that graced her knees. She finished the look with black booties, and diamond studs in her ears. Her curls fell effortlessly over her shoulders.

Koran walked up behind McKinley and wrapped his arms around her slim waist. McKinley smiled as she moved her hair away from her neck. McKinley tilted her head to the right, to expose it to Koran. Like a vampire, Koran was drawn to tasting McKinley's neck. He bent down and planted gentle kisses up and down her neck.

McKinley sighed from pleasure. "That feels so good," she muttered, feeling her head beginning to become light due to the pleasure. She was afraid that she was going to drop her picture, so she quickly placed it down on her kitchen table. As she bent slightly, Koran looked over her shoulder and saw the dress open slightly to expose more of her cleavage. He continued to kiss her neck while he slid one hand into the opening of her dress. "Oh my God," McKinley groaned as Koran began to play with her nipples.

Koran placed his other hand on McKinley's back and gently pushed her further down until her forearms were resting on the kitchen table. She looked back at Koran and their eyes met with a mix of desire and trust embedded in their stare. Koran leaned toward her, and passionately kissed her. McKinley melted while also tooting her booty toward him in preparation of him entering her.

As they kissed, Koran's hands cupped her breasts. From that angle, they felt extremely full and round. Koran relished the feel of her fullness, before he slid his hands down the sides of her body. McKinley laid her head on the table as Koran's hands graced her hips, and then were underneath her dress. She then felt her thong being pulled down her legs, and once they were at her ankles, she stepped out of them.

On his knees, Koran tested her wetness by running his finger up and down her slit. He then pushed her dress on her back to reveal her round ass and juicy pussy. As much as he wanted to bury his penis in it, he wanted to taste it first, and with one motion, his mouth met her lips. McKinley slightly jumped, but then melted again with pleasure as Koran began to eat her pussy from behind. She lifted slightly to allow one of her hands to fondle her own breasts, while the other one stabilized her on the table. Koran varied between flicking his tongue on her clit and sucking on it.

McKinley began to experience wave after wave of pleasure, while her cries of satisfaction were getting louder. McKinley didn't care who heard her, she was in the moment and she didn't feel bad about who knew it.

After she experienced multiple orgasms, Koran rose and took off his black button down Stone Rose shirt. Once McKinley heard him unzip his PRPS jeans, she knew she was in exquisite trouble.

Koran slowly entered her, allowing each inch of himself to enter her and enjoying all of her warmth. One hand traveled up her back and rested in her silky hair, while the other hand rested on her hip. As he began to thrust, McKinley threw her pussy back at him. Each time that their bodies met, it felt as though electricity was being created. Koran began to feel overwhelmed with his emotions. He never thought that anyone after Whitney would create the feelings that he had for her, but McKinley was beginning to fill the void that he felt would always be open. In the time that they'd been together, she reminded him that love was possible, and he wanted to explore that with her.

As the two of them began reaching the finish line together,

Koran was certain that McKinley was who he wanted to be with.

XoXo

Vanessa was sitting in her room, studying when her phone rang. She looked at the caller ID and saw that it was Malik. She was happy, but sad at the same time. She didn't really feel like talking, but she knew that she had to.

"Hey ma," Malik said, happy.

"Hey," Vanessa said, trying to shield her voice from disappointment. She hated what was going on and how she had to play a part, but she knew that she had to, if not she could be in danger.

Malik could hear the trepidation in Vanessa's voice. "What's the problem?"

Vanessa shut her book and walked around her bedroom. There were ribbons, metals, and certificates of her past achievements, and all she wanted to do was to rip them all off the wall. "Nothing, I'm just not feeling too good. You know, the baby," Vanessa rolled her eyes.

Malik immediately felt bad for being so defensive with Vanessa when she first got on the phone. He knew that women's emotions were unpredictable when they were pregnant. "Do you want me to come over? I can bring you whatever you're craving right now."

Vanessa opened her mouth. She didn't know what she was about to say, but she knew what she wanted to say. She wanted to yell at Malik to leave her alone, and to protect himself, but before any words could be uttered, someone knocked on her door. A sudden chill went up her spine and she knew who it was already. He told her that he was coming, but she was never mentally prepared for his arrival.

Vanessa opened her door, and O was standing in the doorway. He smiled at her and walked into her room without being invited.

Vanessa turned her back to him and cradled the phone with both hands. She didn't realize it, but she had started crying. "Nah, I think I'm just going to go to sleep. I'll talk to you tomorrow for your birthday, okay?"

"Alright, bye baby." Malik wasn't satisfied with the conversation, but he knew that he didn't want to stress her or the baby out, so he just decided to leave it alone for now.

"Bye." Vanessa quickly hung up the phone. She put her head down and her shoulders began to heave as she cried.

"Oh boo-fuckin'-hoo, Nessa."

Vanessa turned around and saw that O had spread himself across her bed. She hated seeing him, but she knew she had a debt to pay.

When Vanessa's mother started getting really bad with her drug addiction and couldn't pay, she would offer up Vanessa to the dealers. Vanessa's mother had prostituted her since she was thirteen years old. Vanessa wanted to leave, and tried to leave so many times, but nothing ever panned out. Family members didn't have enough room for her, shelters were full, and she was too embarrassed to tell anyone at school, so she learned to just suck it up and to shut the world out when it was happening. She would use the images of college and owning her own daycare to replace her horrible present, and she strived hard to get herself as close to her goal of leaving her hell-hole situation and never looking back.

But when she found out she was pregnant, she was devastated that all of her plans had been horribly derailed. The same day she found out, her mother offered her to O, and Vanessa finally broke down and told him about the pregnancy.

He told her that he would keep all of the other drug dealers away from her and give her mother whatever she wanted, if she could do something for him.

O wanted more young soldiers on the block, and he personally wanted Malik on there. He knew that if he could get Malik to sling for him that it would be an ultimate payback move to Koran for almost killing him at the club six years ago. But that wasn't it, O wanted more than that. He had a plan to really make Koran suffer, and Vanessa was his key through the entire time. He already knew that Malik had a crush on her from when she was tutoring him, so it was easy to get Malik to wife her up.

O paid for her abortion, as long as Vanessa pretended to be interested in Malik, get him to have sex with her and pretend she was pregnant long enough for him to feel pressured to get on the block. After he was certified, O wanted Vanessa to fake a miscarriage, and then he would wipe all of her mother's debt away. Never again would her mother be able to use her for payment, and O even gave her a free car as collateral, to prove to her that he would help her, as long as she helped him.

The problem was, she really began to care for Malik. He was so nice, genuine, and wanted nothing more but to do right by her. She didn't feel comfortable using him, and luring him into such a horrible situation just so O could get his payback. But she felt like dying every single time that she had to lie under a drug dealer, while he raped her, just so her mother could be reconnected with whatever drug of choice she was on at that time.

"Why are you being so dramatic?" O asked, grabbing a pillow from her bed and tossing it at her.

"I don't think I can do this anymore," Vanessa struggled to speak through sobs.

O looked nonchalantly and shrugged his shoulders. "That's fine, just know that your mother just got another cut today from me, and you know she can't pay…"

Vanessa glared at O, but in his eyes she only saw excitement. Whether she finished screwing over Malik or not, O would eventually get something that he wanted. If she did go through with the plan, then O would be able to get back at Koran. If she didn't, he would rape her. O put himself in a position that no matter what move anyone made, he would always win.

Vanessa dried her tears. "Fine, he should be calling you tomorrow to set up some type of an arrangement. I'll talk him into it."

O clapped his hands together and walked over to Vanessa. He brought her in for a reluctant hug. "That's great, but just know that your credit with me is running thin." O's voice got lower and became sinister, "I mean, you're sitting here, driving that nigga around in the car that I bought you, and you buying him food with my money." Vanessa was terrified, *how often was O watching them?* "Your life is hinged upon what I decide I want to happen to you, okay?" He kissed Vanessa on her forehead and pushed her away. She fell on the dingy carpet in her room. O didn't even look to see if she was okay, or even looked back at her at all once he left. He just walked right out of her room and left the door open.

Vanessa burst into tears. She didn't know how her life had managed to get to this point, but since it was there, she was struggling with how to make things right again. She knew that things were getting out of hand, but she was at the mercy of O, and if she didn't do what he said, she knew that he would probably kill her.

Vanessa dried her tears and stood up. She walked over to her cell phone and dialed Malik's number.

The moment that he answered the phone, Vanessa blurted out, "We need to talk."

"Pimp a nigga out, and treat a lame like a lame."

K. Michelle

"Loyal"

Malik sat at a booth at Dave and Busters looking and feeling very anxious. Every second he sat there he felt like he was about to jump out of his skin. He had too much to do in such a short amount of time.

Koran sat opposite from him and knew that something was bothering him. Koran helped take care of Malik ever since he was a child, and even after he broke up with Trina because she had cheated on him, he still made sure to be in Malik's life. He was emotionally attached to him and wanted to keep him on a straight path. Even though Malik now lived in an upper-class area of St. Louis, Koran still knew how easy it was for a young Black man to fall into the pits of trapping, and how it's even harder to get out of.

"What's on your mind, lil' man?"

Malik look at Koran for a second. It took him a while to register what he had just said to him, his mind was on his conversation with Vanessa the previous night. "Uh... nothing, man. I'm just... nothing, it's nothing."

Koran twisted his top lip, "Nah, I know it's something, because every time I call you lil' man, you go on this tirade about how you're not little anymore, and you about to be driving soon, and all that other bitchness you be talking about." Koran teased, but Malik still looked preoccupied. "But seriously," Koran put all the joking aside and looked Malik straight into his eyes, "what's going on? Is it your girl? Harlow loves her at the daycare center."

Malik looked around, as if to gauge his environment, before he spilled his guts to Koran. "I was just wondering, are you happy with the way that your life is now, or how it was before you went straight?"

Koran sat back in his seat trying to figure out which path this conversation was heading in. "I'm definitely happier now, but why you ask though?"

Malik ran his hands over his face, and then looked back at his soda. "I'm just--," he couldn't dare tell Koran that he was thinking about getting into the trap game, he'd promised him that he never would. But after his phone call with Vanessa last night, he couldn't get it out of his mind. Vanessa's voice broke with fear of the uncertainty of how they could take care of their baby together. Malik didn't want to leave Vanessa out in the cold. He wanted to be a father for his own child, the way that Koran was for him, even though he wasn't his biological father. So when Vanessa started pushing him to go ahead and join a set, just long enough to get some money saved up for the baby, he started considering it. But, he knew that Koran would beat his ass if he found out that he was thinking about going into the same game that Koran left behind six years ago, so he just changed the subject. "It's just Moms, you know? Even though Marcus got all of this money, she never seems happy, and she's been borrowing money from me."

"Word?" Koran grabbed his soda and took a sip from it, oblivious to the relieved look on Malik's face that Koran bought his story. "You know your mama, she never seems satisfied wit' what she has until it's gone."

Malik nodded his head profusely. He had to admit that his mother was extremely flakey, but then he realized that bringing her up was even more of a poor idea, because he couldn't stop hearing O's voice in his head about "taking care of yo' mama." Last time a guy left them they were almost homeless, and if his mother is messing things up again, he's old enough to pick up the slack. *Shit, what am I going to do?* Malik thought, bouncing his leg again.

Koran watched Malik look nervous, and he knew that it wasn't brought on by just his mama's foolishness, but he knew that pressing Malik wasn't going to get him any answers today. "Look man," Koran grabbed a napkin and wiped his hands, "if someone isn't doing right, you can't make them. You can only control you. Be there for your mother, remind her of what's important, and after that it's all up to her. There's nothing else you can do, you understand me?"

Malik felt hopeless, but he didn't want to talk to Koran about it. Koran had his life set up good. He was able to use his drug money to go to college, get some degrees, and set up a couple of businesses. Koran forgot what it was like to struggle. Koran did what he had to do to survive and provide for himself when he was younger. Now Malik has to not only potentially provide for himself, but also for his child. He didn't know why this new Koran was acting all holier than thou, but he knew that the old Koran would understand his plight.

XoXo

McKinley sat on the floor of Koran's house holding a brunette Barbie doll in her hand. The living room table was moved to give more room to McKinley and Harlow to play. *Dear God, how long do I have to keep playing with this girl?* McKinley thought to herself. It wasn't that she didn't like Harlow, it was just that it'd been over an hour, and when she checked her class notes that morning for the professor's class she left early on Friday, her professor had assigned a paper to be due by Monday. She had work to do, and each second that she sat there she felt more anxious.

Harlow was sitting by her Barbie Dream House and had two of the dolls talking to each other. "You want to ride the jeep to the party?" she had one of the dolls ask the other. "Yeah, let's invite Natalie." Harlow turned to McKinley with anticipation. "Natalie?" Harlow directed to McKinley. She began to become even more annoyed that McKinley wasn't paying attention to her. "McKinley!" she finally shouted at her.

McKinley came out of her thoughts and looked surprisingly at Harlow. *Damn, little girl. You didn't have to yell at me.*

"What do you need, Harlow?" She tried to hide her rolling her eyes, but Harlow caught her.

"First, I don't need an attitude," Harlow snipped at McKinley.

Alright, little girl. Damn, McKinley thought.

"Second, I need you to sit right here," Harlow patted the floor next to her. "Natalie needs to come to the party with them." Harlow turned her back to McKinley, swinging her long ponytails behind her.

I don't have time for this. McKinley walked over to Harlow and gave her Natalie. "Why don't I put the pizza in the oven?"

The hurt expression that Harlow had when she was given her Barbie doll back was replaced with joy. Harlow got up and started dancing, "Oh yeah! Pizza!"

McKinley couldn't help but laugh. Though Harlow could be a handful, she was still a pretty good child. *Maybe I can do this,* McKinley thought, imagining her life with Koran and Harlow as she scooped her laptop in her arms and carried it to the kitchen.

McKinley put her laptop on the table and opened it. She typed in her password to unlock it and then went to the freezer to pull out a pizza.

"McKinley, can I have a soda, please?" Harlow bounded into the room, with the Barbie dolls still attached to her hands, still pretending like they're talking to each other.

McKinley smiled at her. "Sure, what kind?"

"Strawberry, please." Harlow smiled while pretending like the dolls were walking from one end of the table to the other.

McKinley pulled a strawberry soda out of the fridge, and grabbed a cup. "Let's split it, okay?"

Harlow was still preoccupied with her Barbies, "Okay."

McKinley poured half in a cup and handed it to Harlow, and then she took a sip from the can. She placed the can on the countertop and started looking in the cabinets for a pizza pan. "Harlow, where does your dad—"

"Uh oh," Harlow's voice was small, but full of fear.

McKinley turned around and saw that Harlow had knocked over her soda right onto McKinley's opened laptop. McKinley quickly ran over to the laptop and turned it upside down. "What the fuck, Harlow?! What did you do?!" McKinley didn't realize that she was yelling or cursing, but she was furious.

"I don't know, I was just playing with my Barbies and I wanted to look at your computer—"

"So you dump a whole fucking cup of soda on my fucking computer?! What is wrong with you?!" McKinley knew that she should have stopped, but she couldn't. She quickly took the battery out of the laptop and then grabbed some paper towels and began to wipe off her laptop, completely ignoring the puddle on the table. "I mean, seriously, Harlow! You could have ruined my laptop! Like what is wrong with you?"

McKinley was yelling so loudly that she didn't even hear the garage door open.

Harlow started crying, "I didn't mean to—"

"I know that you didn't mean to, but what am I gonna do if my fuckin' laptop is broken?"

"You can start by stop yelling at my daughter!" Koran's voice bellowed through the house, stopping McKinley in mid-motion. She'd never seen Koran so angry before, she actually felt frightened. The look that he gave her was one of wanting to grab her by the collar of her shirt, and he probably would have, if Harlow hadn't run up to him, crying. His face softened when he saw how upset she was.

"I'm sorry, Daddy. I didn't mean to spill the soda on her computer, please don't punish me." Harlow began to heave due to her heavy sobs.

McKinley felt less than a person, she felt like a monster, *how could I be so mean to a six year old? She didn't mean to do it,* McKinley completely overreacted.

Koran picked Harlow up and hugged her tightly. "I know, baby, it's okay," he soothed her and rubbed his hand over her hair. He grabbed a napkin from the table and began to dry the tears and snot off of Harlow's face. Once he was done he placed her down in front of him. "Are you okay?"

"Yeah," she sheepishly smiled at her father, and then looked at McKinley. "I'm sorry, McKinley."

McKinley was silently watching up until that time, but then a tear rolled down her cheek. "I know you are, I'm sorry for yelling at you."

Koran didn't look at McKinley and picked Harlow up again. "Why don't you go upstairs to play with your dolls, while I clean up this mess, okay?"

Harlow smiled at him, "Okay, Daddy. Just hurry up, okay? I want you to watch a movie with me, will you?"

Koran kissed Harlow on the cheek. "I definitely will." He put her down and she bounced toward the stairs.

Koran watched as Harlow went up the stairs and into her room.

"I am so sorry," McKinley pleaded.

Koran turned to McKinley with a look of anger and disgust at her. "You're fuckin' right you're sorry. Why in the hell were you fuckin' yelling at my kid?" Koran approached her.

"I—I—I'm just so sorry, I lost it, I didn't mean to. She spilled the soda on my laptop and I had a paper to do, and I just… I'm so sorry, Koran."

Koran looked at McKinley's face and could tell that she truly was sorry, but that was his daughter. Harlow came before anyone else in the world, and if McKinley couldn't control her emotions around her, then they couldn't be together.

Koran couldn't even bring himself to say anything else to her. He just walked around her, grabbed some paper towels and began wiping up the spilled soda. McKinley rushed over to help him. He wanted to tell her that she didn't have to, or to just go home, but he was afraid that the moment he opened his mouth he was going to say something that he couldn't take back, so he just remained quiet.

Once the table and the floor were cleaned, McKinley turned to Koran. He was still silent. He hardly looked at her while they cleaned. *I wish he would just say something to me.* "I guess I'll go home."

"Alright." She prayed for him to say something and the moment he did, his words seemed so heavy and flat. She didn't know what to say or what to think. His face was stone, rigid. It didn't show any signs of what he was thinking, and that scared her even more.

"Okay, bye." McKinley didn't realize that she had whispered it until it seemed like her words were just hanging out of her mouth, like a fishing lure, hoping to catch some type of salutation from Koran, but it never came. She grabbed her things and left, leaving her words the only indication that she was there.

"I am a sinner, who's probably gonna sin again."

Kendrick Lamar
"Bitch, Don't Kill My Vibe"

McKinley stood in front of the door. She was nervous as hell, and looking at the door, she wondered if she could actually do what she was about to do. A car drove in front of the house and she turned to watch it go down the street, *lucky bastard*, she thought to herself. *Let me stop being a pussy and just ring the doorbell.* McKinley didn't want to, but she knew that if she didn't people would start looking and someone was bound to call the cops on her for looking like a weirdo. After one more sigh, she rang the doorbell. *Dear God, this is going to be a mess*, she thought as she heard heavy footsteps approaching the door.

The heavy oak door opened and McKinley's mother, Denise, poked her head out the door. A look of suspicion and surprise filled her face. "Hey hun, come on in."

McKinley forced a smile on her face and followed her mother in. The house still looked pretty much the same that it had when she grew up there, except there seemed to be a slight layer of dust on the plastic that covered the furniture in the living room.

McKinley followed her mother into the den where she had an episode of "Judge Judy" paused.

"So what's going on, baby?" Denise asked her.

She didn't want to talk to her mother about this, but she knew she didn't have anyone else to talk to about it. Kristen would have just made fun of the situation, and Koran still hadn't contacted her and it had been two days since it happened.

McKinley sighed, "I think I really messed up," McKinley could feel the tears begin to line her eyes. "I was babysitting for Koran—"

"His daughter, right?" Denise asked, leaning over to the table and taking a handful of nuts from the candy dish she had ever since McKinley was a child.

McKinley rolled her eyes, "Yeah. Well, his daughter spilled a soda on my laptop and before I knew it, I just started *yelling* at her."

"Oh, no," Denise placed her hand on her chest, as if she was trying to protect her heart from breaking.

Tears began to fall down McKinley's face, and she buried her face into her hands. "I don't know what's wrong with me, but I think I messed up Mom."

Denise began to rub McKinley's back, trying to comfort her, but Denise knew that no matter what she did she couldn't stop her daughter's heart from breaking.

"I mean," McKinley tried to speak through sobs, "after all of that… garbage I went through with Jamil, I finally found someone who treated me like I actually mattered. Someone who was there for me, and I messed it up by yelling at his daughter."

Denise brought her daughter's head to her chest, and she

slightly rocked as she tried to comfort her. "It's okay, being a parent is hard, it happens. You're gonna lose your cool, but it's a learning experience. You'll get it."

McKinley rose up from her mother's bosom, wiped her face and then looked at her. "But, what if I don't... want to?"

Denise looked at her daughter surprised. "Wait, what?"

McKinley looked away from her mother. She knew that once she said what she was going to say it was going to make her mother upset at her. "I mean, as much as I care for Koran, I don't know if I'm ready to be with his daughter. She's a really sweet girl, but I don't know if I can handle being around children right now."

Denise took a deep breath. She knew that what she was about to say to her daughter was harsh, but it needed to be said. "What in the hell is wrong with you?"

Shock covered McKinley's face. She'd only heard her mother swear a handful of times, and never did those times happen at her. "What do you mean what's wrong with me?"

"You claim you like this man, could fall in love with him, but you don't want to be bothered with the daughter? This isn't a mix and match deal, honey. Wherever he goes, she will go because they are tied together. You can't just pick and choose what parts of his life you want to be involved in. If you want to be with him then you have to accept him for how he is completely. Don't start saying some of that stupid stuff to him, or to anyone else for that matter." Denise reached for another handful of peanuts and popped them in her mouth. "People are going to start thinking I didn't raise you right, and I know I did!"

McKinley was shocked at what her mother said, but she knew that it was right. "But honestly, I might not even have a choice. I haven't talked to him in two days—"

"You're damn right he hasn't talked to you! Do you know what I would do if anyone ever yelled at you?"

McKinley rolled her eyes. "What Mom?"

"Kicked they ass." McKinley burst into laughter. Before this time, her relationship with her mother was always telling her what she was doing wrong, and it created a void between them. Now, her mother was actually being emotionally help-ful. "I'm serious, McKinley. A parent will always choose their children before anyone else, and we will always feel protective over our children. Especially if you're a single parent. Once your father left and it was just me and you, you had to come first; and that poor man lost his wife at the same time that his daughter was born. He's been through something, and the only bright light during that time was his daughter, so she's more precious to him than those crazy looking clothes you're always wearing but can hardly pronounce."

McKinley stared at her mother. She knew her mother was right, but she still didn't know if she was ready for what being a parent would entail. "I mean, I do feel like I'm beginning to love him."

"Well," Denise grabbed her DVR's remote control, "stop being a prima donna and accept that man and all of his baggage, because Lord knows he did the same for you."

McKinley reached forward and grabbed a handful of nuts as well.

"Now, you wanna watch the rest of this "Judge Judy" with me? It's a good episode." Denise looked at the remote control, trying to find the play button.

McKinley shrugged her shoulders, "Sure. Why not? Just... why not?"

XoXo

Koran sat in front of an attractive light skinned woman. She wore her auburn natural tightly coiled hair in a poof on top of her head. He'd just hired her as a new cashier for his store. "Do you mind starting tomorrow? Or is that too soon."

The woman shrugged her shoulders, "That's fine. It's not too early," she smiled at him, but before he could say anything back the door flew open.

McKinley walked in, and immediately stopped when she saw the woman staring back at her. "Oh, I'm sorry, I didn't know that you were meeting with someone." She tried to walk back out.

"McKinley, no, go ahead and stay. I was just finishing preparing Ashley for her first day on the job tomorrow."

Both Koran and Ashley stood up. She shook Koran's hand and then headed toward the door. She stopped in front of McKinley and shook her hand, "I'm Ashley, nice to meet you."

"Hi, Ashley," she said half-heartedly. McKinley was too preoccupied with what she planned to talk to Koran about to be introducing herself to some broad.

Ashley left, and then McKinley and Koran stood there, looking at each other.

Finally, Koran broke the ice, "You wanna have a seat?"

McKinley went over to the seat and plopped down, relieved that Koran was finally speaking to her. "Look, I—"

"Nah, let me," Koran interrupted her. "I know that parenting can be a handful, especially for people who aren't used to it, or ready for it. I know that your reaction was a gut one, but I have to let you know that I can't have anyone talking to my daughter like that."

"I know," McKinley said as she scooted to the edge of her seat. "That's why I came to apologize. I don't know what came over me, but it wasn't okay that it happened, and I'm sorry for it."

"Thank you for apologizing," Koran sat back in his seat and looked McKinley over. He did miss her, but he had to take a step back for a minute. McKinley wore a yellow scoop neck shirt, with dark blue skinny jeans and black leather riding boots. She looked beautiful as her hair was braided in a side ponytail that cascaded over her shoulders.

"No problem, I was in the wrong. Is Harlow okay? Does she still like me?"

Koran laughed, "She thinks you're kinda mean now, but you'll just have to work on her." He stopped smiling for a second and looked at McKinley seriously. "You do know that she's not going anywhere, right? You're gonna have to deal wit' her as long as you're dealing wit' me."

McKinley sighed. "Yeah, I know, but I feel like you accepted me for who I was and all of the crazy things that came along with me, so I can do the same for you." McKinley stood up and leaned over the desk to give him a kiss. Koran met her in the center and the two kissed. "You wanna go to lunch, I have an hour and a half before class."

Koran shook his head, "Nah, I got some paperwork to do. It's so much to file and fill out with a new employee, it's crazy. But why don't I meet up with you this weekend? We have inventory here tonight, too."

McKinley's face dropped. She wanted for things to be back to normal with Koran, and she wanted to really reunite that night, but she guessed she didn't mind if they had to wait until the weekend. She was just happy that he forgave her. Plus, Kristen was coming into town, so it would give her some time to catch up with her friend.

XoXo

McKinley left out from the back of his store and then exited out the front. McKinley was halfway to her car when she
heard a woman calling her name. She looked and it was Ashley
coming up behind her.

"Hey McKinley, wait!"

What does this bitch want? McKinley thought, alarmed.

"Hey, umm... this is gonna sound weird, but do you want
to do lunch with me?" Ashley held a very intense gaze on
McKinley.

McKinley felt awkward, "I don't know, I was planning on
leaving."

Ashley's eyes fell to the ground, "Well, I understand. It's
just that, I just moved here and I'm hoping to meet some new
people, you know? But I understand if you don't want to do it."

McKinley wanted to yell *of course I don't want to do it!*
I don't even know you! But she didn't. Instead she looked at
Ashley and saw how vulnerable she was, and decided to lower
her walls and go with Ashley. *I mean, it's only lunch, right?*

XoXo

The two women sat opposite from each other at Olive Gar-
den. McKinley had her fork in her hand, tapping the handle of
it on the table, while Ashley looked at McKinley calmly. *Why*

– 243 –

did she want to go out with me? McKinley thought.

As if reading her mind, Ashley began talking: "I'm sorry for approaching you that way, it's just... I just moved here and didn't know anyone. You seemed like a nice and pretty woman."

McKinley softened up after that compliment. "Damn, you don't need to tell me I'm sexy, I already know it," McKinley joked. Ashley smiled slightly and then looked down and began playing with her napkin. "So, where are you from?"

Ashley looked up at McKinley with tears in her eyes. "I just moved from Atlanta, actually, I've been moving around a lot. My fiancé was a soldier. He got distracted while in the line of duty and died in battle, leaving me a single mother."

McKinley's mouth dropped open. *Damn, I thought I had it bad.* "I'm so sorry to hear that. How are you dealing with it?"

Ashley sighed and began twisting her cup of water on the table, "I mean, it's hard, especially being a single mom. In fact, I left my child with my parents while I try to set things up. Me and my guy had our own business, and I'm just trying to work to get some money and get it back up and running, and I'm hoping to do it here."

"But why St. Louis? What type of business?" McKinley took a sip of water. She felt in awe of Ashley. Not only was she not deterred by her loss, but she was empowered by it. *If she can make things work with her kid and no man, I can do this with Koran and Harlow.*

"It was a distributing firm. We did a lot of exporting and importing for businesses, handling merchandise and sending it back out to distributors. It wasn't really glamorous, but we made a lot of money." Ashley said, beginning to perk up reminiscing on her past. "We had firms in Florida, California, and Atlanta, but I was more so a silent partner, so when he died the business went down with him. But I found an investor in St. Louis who's willing to work with me, and I know this business back and forth, so I know that I can pick it back up once I get some money."

"What part of Florida was your business in?" McKinley asked, eyeing an approaching waiter. *Please let that be my soup and salad, I am starving*, McKinley thought.

"Miami actually, I spent some time there. I really liked it," Ashley said, almost whimsically.

McKinley's eyes lit up. "I used to live there, and sometimes I miss it. You know, I have a friend who's coming to visit from Miami. We're just going out dancing on Thursday night, you wanna come?"

Ashley's face lit up, "Sure! Thanks for the invite."

"No problem, now when is our food coming? I am so hungry and I need to head back to class," McKinley began looking around again while Ashley stared at her.

"You own my heart, he just renting."

Nicki Minaj ft. Chris Brown

"Right By Your Side"

Malik's phone buzzed in his pocket during class. It was ten in the morning and he was in his second class of the day. He didn't want his teacher to confiscate his phone, so he tried to ignore it, but it kept on buzzing. *Who's trying to contact me right now?* Whoever it was, they would hang up and then call right back. *This shit better be an emergency*, he thought as he raised his hand.

The teacher was writing on the board about the devastating results of the Stock Market Crash that led to the Great Depression in the 1930s. Mrs. Raines turned and saw Malik's hand up. "Yes, Malik?"

"Can I go to the bathroom?"

Mrs. Raines walked over to her desk and wrote him a hall pass, "Hurry up, this is a lot of information."

"So don't be stinkin' up the bathroom for thirty minutes," a student in the back of the room shouted. The class burst into applause and laughter.

"Matt, calm down," Mrs. Raines scolded the student. Malik walked up to Mrs. Raines and got the pass from her. On his way out he discretely put his middle finger up at Matt.

"Ohhhhh!" The students yelled in unison.

"Alright, son," Matt nodded back at Malik.

"Class! Quiet down or it's a pop quiz!"

The students quieted down as Malik exited the classroom and headed to the bathroom. His phone vibrated and buzzed in his pocket while he was approaching the bathroom.

Once he got into the bathroom, he entered a stall, pulled his phone out of his pocket, and saw that he had four missed calls from O.

Malik rolled his eyes and leaned against the stall's wall, *this nigga*. He dialed O back.

"Lil nigga, why didn't you answer my fuckin' phone calls?" O yelled the moment he answered the phone.

Malik rolled his eyes and suppressed the urge to curse him out and hang up on him. "I was in class," Malik uttered through gritted teeth.

"Nigga, I need you. One of my other soldiers can't be on the block today, I need you to take his spot," O said between handfuls of potato chips.

"I can't just leave school," Malik whispered, afraid that one of the teachers or security guards that patrolled the hallways were going to hear him. He wasn't even supposed to have his phone on in school and he knew he could get in trouble having it. "Plus, I don't even have my stuff," Malik was hoping that would be enough reason for O to find someone else to work the corner for him.

"Didn't I tell you to always keep it on you? You never know when you can sell!" O's voice was beginning to become sinister. "Look, I'm not arguing with yo' bitch-ass, you were the one callin' and cryin' to me about how you needed money.

Now that you have the opportunity, you wanna bitch out? Nah, nigga, that's not how this game goes. Go home, get your product and I'll pick you up in twenty minutes and put you where you're supposed to be."

Before Malik could say anything O hung up on him. "Shit!" Malik yelled louder than he realized.

He heard rapid footsteps approaching the bathroom. "Who's in there?" an authoritative male voice yelled.

"It's Malik Lewis," he called out from the stall.

"You gotta hall pass?"

"Yeah."

"Well, hurry up, and stop cursing," the voice reprimanded him.

"Okay," Malik flushed the toilet to make the security guard leave. Malik waited until he heard the guard leave and his footsteps were down the hall.

Malik exited the stall and looked at himself in the mirror above the sinks. *How did I get into this shit?* Malik sighed and left the bathroom. After a quick look down the hall to make sure the coast was clear, Malik walked to the closest exit and then headed home.

XoXo

Malik entered the front door of his house and went up the stairs. His mind was racing and all he knew was that he needed to find his stash and be outside by the time O got there.

He went into his room and went into the back of his closet and got an old pair of sneakers that he hollowed the bottom out of. He removed the sole to reveal his stash of merchandise, some crack, heroin, and meth. He grabbed the bags and vials and stuffed them in his pocket.

Malik started walking toward the stairwell when he heard a thumping noise coming from the master bedroom. *What's that?* He thought as he approached his parents' door. "Mama," he called out.

"Malik?" Trina's voice was filled with panic.

Malik heard the rustling of covers and something falling and breaking. He ran to her room, "Mama, you okay?" He burst through the door thinking that he was going to find his mother hurt, but instead saw her and a White guy naked on the bed, scrambling to cover themselves up with the sheets.

"Don't come in here! What are you doing?" Trina yelled at Malik.

Malik quickly averted his eyes. He wasn't expecting to see his mother having sex with some random dude in the middle of the morning. He quickly shut the door and speed walked to the staircase.

He heard the door to his mother's room open but he refused to look back, he just kept on walking. The sound of O honking his horn was heard and Malik couldn't believe that he was relieved to actually go with O.

"Malik, wait!" Trina ran behind him. "Wait, let's talk about this."

Malik refused to stop walking, he just wanted to get out and forget what he just saw, but Trina caught up with him and grabbed him by the shoulder. He turned around and saw that she had her robe on. She grabbed his hand, stopping him from walking away.

"Malik, please!"

"Please what? I don't understand what you expect me to say?" Malik asked. O honked his horn again, impatiently. Malik looked toward the door and Trina followed his glance.

"Wait a second, why aren't you at school? Who's blowing their car horn?"

Malik began to feel frazzled. "Look, Mama, if you don't want me to say anything to Marcus, then fine, I won't. But I don't want to talk about this ever again. I gotta go."

Trina let go of his hand and Malik left out of the front door, not looking back or saying "bye." Trina walked to the window and peered out to see whose car it was. The moment she saw the Bentley Mulsanne she knew it was O's. *That son of a bitch,* Trina thought getting angry.

XoXo

"Are you going to miss me tonight?" McKinley teased while putting a dress in front of her body while posing in the mirror.

"You know I am, but I want you to have fun tonight," Koran said, his voice echoing through her phone's speakers.

"You too. I'm sorry I can't make the gala tonight, but—"

"But ya girl has to show me around your town," Kristen butted in the conversation.

Koran laughed. "Nah, I understand, just take care of my girl, a'ight?"

"Yeah, yeah, this heffa won't be doin' nothing crazy tonight. Not while I'm around." Kristen joked as McKinley walked over and gently pushed her.

"Alright, I'm almost at the event, I'll see y'all ladies later."

McKinley walked over to the phone and took it off of speaker phone. "Alright baby, 'bye."

Kristen started making gagging noises, and McKinley flipped her off.

"Bye, baby." Koran said and the two disconnected their phone call.

"Y'all two acting like y'all will never see each other again. Y'all ain't on the Titanic, bitch. You'll see him later!" Kristen teased while looking in the mirror that McKinley was posing in earlier.

"Yeah, yeah, bitch. Don't hate, you know you wish you

had a man like mine." McKinley picked up her dress and booty bumped Kristen from in front of the mirror.

"Keep on teasing and I'll steal yours." The two friends laughed. "But seriously, I'm glad that you're doing good here, and it seems like Koran is a good dude."

McKinley took off her jeans and shirt so she could slip the dress over her head. "I'm glad too, because after dealing with Jamil's fraudulent ass, my asshole quotient was already filled. I didn't have any more room for any extra foolishness."

Kristen applied another coat of her Dior lipstick, "Honey, I feel you. These niggas act like they don't know how to act anymore, but you found one that's good, so make sure you keep him."

McKinley smoothed the black slip dress with her hands to get the wrinkles out. "I'm gonna try my best."

"Well try harder, and stop cursing out his child!" Kristen yelled at McKinley. McKinley cut her eyes at Kristen. "Hey, just a thought," Kristen shrugged her shoulders. Kristen was wearing a long sleeved purple jumpsuit. Her bob was sleek, and accented her cheekbones.

"Don't worry, I'll just stick to cursin' at you, motherfuck-er," McKinley said while slipping into a black leather motor-cycle jacket. "You ready to go?"

"Yeah, let's see what this ho-dunk town has to offer."

McKinley opened the door for Kristen and she walked

out, before she locked the door on her way out. "Hey, don't be talking about my town."

As they walked toward the elevator, Kristen began smoothing her hair with her hand. "Girl, you know it ain't nothing compared to Miami, but I'll give it a try." Kristen pressed the down button on the elevator. When it arrived they both got on while McKinley pressed the button for the parking garage. "Do you ever get scared living on your own?"

McKinley adjusted her jacket, "I used to, until I got that fire."

Kristen's eyes widened and she took a step back from McKinley. "Whaaaat?" she joked. "I thought you hated guns."

"I did, before Jamil was killed. After that, a bitch got paranoid. Especially since it was my first time living on my own."

"Really?"

"Yeah, I went from living with my mama, to Jamil, to being on my own. I thought about getting a dog, but I don't have the patience to take care of something else, I'm just really learning now to take care of myself." The elevator doors opened at the parking garage and the two women sauntered off and headed toward McKinley's car.

"Well, you're doing a great job so far, bitch." Kristen said, waiting for McKinley to unlock her door.

"You gonna keep on," McKinley opened up her door and unlocked Kristen's door, "I'm not gonna be too many more bitches," she teased.

Kristen grinned at her friend. "Please, bitch, you gonna find out that I'm not the one, two, three *or* the four." The two laughed. "Now who are we meeting again?"

"This chick named Ashley, she's new in town and wanted to have someone to hang out with." McKinley said keeping her eyes on the road.

"She cool?"

"Yeah, but," McKinley stopped herself, trying to find a good way to describe Ashley. "She can give off this intense vibe, you know? Like, she stares a lot."

"She probably trying to find a way to get the cooch," Kristen cackled.

"You crazy. Don't go being raunchy and scaring the poor girl off, she ain't got too many friends here yet."

Kristen flipped open the vanity visor and checked out her reflection. "Probably because she keeps on scaring people away with her "The Ring" stare."

The two laughed as McKinley continued to drive.

XoXo

Koran walked around the conference room of the Renaissance Hotel off of the Landing. Around him were about a hundred people who were investors, staff members, and donators to his cancer center called "Hopes." He opened it in honor of his late wife, and he was pleased that it had been going strong so far.

He was engaged in a conversation with an investor when he felt a hand tap him on the shoulder. He turned and saw Trina and Marcus.

So much time had passed, and he and Trina were finally able to peacefully coexist, and her husband, Marcus handled the insurance for the Hopes' building. Koran excused himself from his previous conversation and turned to give them his full attention. "Hi, good to see you two."

"Likewise," Marcus said, shaking Koran's hand. "I must say, each year things seem to be getting better and better for you."

"It's all God, my brother," Koran said. "Can I get you two a drink?"

"I'll just have a white wine," Marcus said, turning to Trina to get her drink order.

"I don't know what I want. I'll go to the bar with Koran," Trina said, giving Marcus a quick peck on the cheek.

I hope she's not on some bullshit tonight, Koran thought as the two walked to the bartender area in the right corner of the room. They stood in line to wait to be served.

"I gotta talk to you about something."

"What's up?"

"It's about Malik, I saw him with O the other day."

Koran looked at Trina, a look of panic covered his face. *That's what was bothering him*, he thought. "Did he say anything to you?"

"He refused," she said looking around. She saw that Marcus had started a new conversation with his back turned to her. "You're the only one who can talk some sense into him, and stop him if he's doing what I think he's doing." The line moved forward, and Trina and Koran shuffled ahead.

"I'll talk to him," Koran looked ahead. He could tell this wasn't the end of the conversation. He was with Trina for four years, and he could just feel she had something else planned to talk about.

"Thank you, Koran. You know," she looked around again to make sure that Marcus wasn't looking their way. "You were the only man that I really did love."

It was finally their time to deliver their drink orders. "A white wine, and a glass of champagne." Koran ordered.

"I'll have a champagne as well," Trina told the bartender. The bartender nodded and turned to grab three flutes.

"Trina, don't start with that bullshit."

"What bullshit? What do you mean?" She tried to play dumb.

"You know exactly what I'm talking about, and this is not the time or the place for it." Koran said, avoiding eye contact with her. He knew that he couldn't give her an inch.

"After all of these years, you don't think that you still feel it? I mean, you still in Malik's life."

The bartender placed the three drinks on the countertop, and Koran grabbed the wine and champagne, and Trina grabbed her champagne then they began walking slowly back toward Marcus.

"No, I don't feel anything. I thought we both moved on. I mean, damn, you're married. When are you going to get it together?"

Trina stopped walking and looked at Koran. "What do you mean, get it together?"

Koran finally looked at her, "You know exactly what I mean. You mess things up for yourself. Whenever you're in a good situation you always try to ruin it, it's like you're addicted to drama or something. You need to get to the point where you can just be happy where you are and wit' who you're wit' instead of always trying to find forever."

Marcus approached Trina and Koran.

"Hey, here's your wine," Koran said, handing him the glass. "Now if you two don't mind, I have a few more hands to shake." Koran shook Marcus's hand, "Nice seeing you again, man."

"You too," Marcus smiled. He looked down at Trina and saw that she had tears in her eyes. Koran walked away and Marcus turned to her. "Are you okay?"

Trina snapped out of her feelings and smiled back at Marcus. "Yeah, I'm just happy to see you," she kissed him on the cheek and locked arms with him. The two walked away together and engaged in another conversation with the Mayor and his wife.

"That girl looks familiar.
Real recognize real, that's
familiar."

Ty Dollar ft. 2 Chainz
"Familiar"

McKinley and Kristen walked into the Pepper Lounge off of Locust Street. They were engulfed in a sea of red lights and mahogany booths, covered with leather. There was an open dance floor filled with people drinking and dancing while listening to the band Dirty Muggs. Dirty Muggs were popular in St. Louis for their remarkable covers of popular songs and their own good songs.

"Alright," Kristen said, nodding at the cover of "Blurred Lines." "Dude sounds just like Robin Thicke!" McKinley turned to her and nodded.

They both looked around trying to find Ashley, when McKinley saw her. Ashley was standing by the bar, staring at McKinley and Kristen intently. Her natural hair was in a beautiful, wild afro, with a few tendrils that framed her face. McKinley elbowed Kristen in the ribs and then gestured in Ashley's direction.

Kristen bent down and whispered in McKinley's ear. "You weren't joking with the staring. That shit is creepy."

McKinley threw her head back and laughed. "Be nice," McKinley warned as the two approached Ashley. "Hey Ashley, this is my friend Kristen," McKinley tried to yell over the music. Ashley smiled and shook Kristen's hand.

Kristen tried to yell to Ashley, but Ashley shrugged and pointed to her ear while shaking her head, telling Kristen that she couldn't hear her.

For some reason, Kristen felt incredibly uncomfortable around Ashley. She couldn't put her finger on it, but there was something in her telling her to watch her closely and to not trust her.

XoXo

"Woo, I have to say, I didn't think that I would have fun in your little hick town, but I surprisingly did," Kristen said while slipping her Balenciaga heels off.

"I told you the S.T.L. could be live," McKinley said poking her head out of her bathroom. She was washing the make-up off of her face, and was in the process of massaging the cleanser in circles over her face.

"You were right, I had fun. Except," Kristen stopped herself as she tried to find the right words to say.

"Except what?" McKinley said over the loud sound of her faucet as she rinsed the cleanser off of her face. Once she was done she grabbed her towel and dabbed at her face, and then grabbed her nighttime moisturizer and walked into her room where Kristen was sitting on the bed. "What's on yo' mind, girl?"

"Ashley," Kristen said while twisting her lips up and shaking her head. "She kinda creeped me out." Kristen turned to McKinley while she massaged the moisturizer on her face. "You didn't pick up a weird vibe from her?"

McKinley leaned against her door frame and really thought about it. "I mean, kinda, but once she told me about her life I kinda felt a little sad for her, you know?"

"I just can't put my finger on it. It's like I met her before or something." Kristen unzipped her bodysuit and stood up to let it fall off of her shoulders.

"You probably did, she said she spent some time in Miami. Y'all probably got into an argument at a club and you cut her down to size with yo' big mouth and then dismissed her," McKinley joked.

Kristen laughed as she pulled her night shirt over her head. "You're right. You know that I can forget a motherfucka that crosses me in a second."

McKinley climbed on the right side of her bed while Kristen climbed in on the left. "I hope you don't mind my alarm in the morning. I got class, but I'll be back by like four."

"Girl, I won't be paying attention to that punk-ass alarm. I'll probably sleep right through it," Kristen said while turning her back to McKinley, getting comfortable.

"Alright now, don't start complaining when I start getting ready in the morning, talking 'bout how I'm waking you up. You can sleep in until I get back."

"Well let me get some sleep now, trick," Kristen joked.

"Alright, bitch." McKinley laughed. "Goodnight," she turned her lamp off.

"Goodnight."

"Everything that I
prayed for.
God's gift, I wish I
woulda prayed more."
Jay Z
"Glory"

Koran was driving around South St. Louis. These were his old stomping grounds. From his teenage years to his early twenties, Koran was posted up on some of these same corners, slingin' whatever people wanted. Delivering what people felt like they needed, something to soothe their souls, but also kill their bodies. This was where Koran grew up, was raised, became a man, and then a boss.

Koran looked in vain for Malik. He'd texted him multiple times and Malik wasn't answering him back. *Where is he?* Right when he was beginning to feel like he wasn't going to find him, his phone rang. He looked and saw that it was Malik. Koran quickly answered the call. "Malik, where are you?"

"Nah, this ain't Malik," O's voice rang through his ears.

"Motherfucker! Where's Malik, bitch boy?" Koran yelled looking around, trying to see if he could see O's Bentley.

"Please, Koran, that's not how you speak to your old business partner," O was condescending and enjoying every second of the conversation.

"Bitch nigga, you were never my business partner. I ran *you*, remember that! And if it wasn't for people stopping me, you were going to die that night at the club," Koran said, circling the corner. He knew that O had to be somewhere around watching him. Koran wanted to find him first and finish what he should have done years before, before people intervened. "Every time you take a breath, thank me, because you were supposed to die, bitch!"

"I want you to think about that the next time you see your daughter," O said, and then disconnected the call. He turned off Malik's cell phone.

Koran's eyes immediately filled up with tears as he headed toward Harlow's daycare. "Oh my God, this nigga betta not had!" He kept chanting to himself as he ran red lights and stop signs to get to Harlow's daycare.

When he finally arrived, he jumped out of the car while it was still running. He ran into the building and looked around the room. The daycare owner and Vanessa were working with a group of children. The daycare owner approached him, "Mr. McKnight, nice to see you today!" Koran turned to her, and her smiled disappeared when she saw the bewildered look on his face. "My God, what's wrong?"

"I want to see Harlow, right now!" he shouted. The owner looked over at Vanessa and Vanessa approached him. "Vanessa, where's my daughter?"

Vanessa looked away, her heart was pounding in her chest as she had to fight the chunks from rising in her chest. She felt like she was about to vomit in fear. "A woman picked her up, she said you okayed it," Vanessa recited the story that O told her to say.

Koran's voice rose higher. The children around began to become frightened. "What woman?" He grabbed Vanessa by the collar, while the daycare owner tried to intervene.

"Mr. McKnight, please! You're scaring the children!"

"Who took my child?" Tears began to pour from Koran's eyes. He'd never felt more frightened and helpless in his entire life.

"A woman named McKinley," Vanessa said. The words barely came out of her mouth as she shook in fear.

Koran let go of Vanessa's shirt and ran out of the building to his car while simultaneously dialing McKinley's number.

XoXo

McKinley was standing in line at the University's Café, waiting to order a cappuccino. *I knew I shouldn't have went out with Kristen's wild ass. I can barely stay awake now*, she thought as she looked up at the menu. Her phone rang and she looked down and saw that it was Koran. She smiled as she answered the phone. "Hey baby," she cooed into the phone.

"Where's Harlow!" He shouted into the phone, scaring McKinley. His voice was so loud that many people standing next to her heard him and looked at her, concerned.

McKinley stepped out of line and off to the side. "Baby, I don't know, what's going on?"

"The daycare said that you picked her up, where is she?" McKinley had never heard such panic in Koran's voice and it scared her.

"No, I've been in class. I haven't left campus all day."

Koran broke down on the phone. His sobs were excruciating for McKinley to hear. She felt helpless and couldn't imagine how Koran felt.

At that same time, she got a notification. She looked at her phone and saw that Kristen texted her.

From: Kristen

Girl, why is crazy lookin' Ashley knocking on you door with a little girl?

Sent: Today, 3:23pm

"Oh my God!" McKinley yelled.

"What?" Koran yelled back at her, he didn't realize that his anxiety could be compounded, but it was by the way McKinley yelled.

"I think that Ashley has Harlow. Kristen just texted me saying that she's knocking on my apartment door and she has a little girl with her."

Koran was filled with a sense of relief and confusion. He was glad that he might have found Harlow, but *why did Ashley have her?* "I'm almost at your college. Meet me in front of the Student Union and I'll drive you over to your place, okay?"

"Yeah, and I'll tell Kristen to let them in, so they can't go anywhere."

"Okay," and Koran hung up the phone.

McKinley texted Kristen to let her know to let them into

the apartment.

From: Kristen
Alright, but I'm about to get your gun incase anything
pops off.
Sent: Today, 3:27

Before McKinley could respond, she heard someone honking at her anxiously. She saw Koran and she ran to his car. She
jumped in and before she could properly shut the door he took
off, heading to her apartment.

"Fucker never loved us.
You ain't know, now
you know now."

Drake

"Worst Behavior"

By the time they pulled up to McKinley's apartment, Koran had stopped crying. They went to park, when Koran stopped the car abruptly. "Motherfucker!" He yelled and stopped the car, and jumped out without taking his keys out.

"Koran!" McKinley yelled after him. She slid into the driver's side while Koran ran into the building. McKinley parked the car and got out and ran inside. From the corner of her eye, she spotted a lavish Bentley Mulsanne in the parking lot. The car seemed to stick out like a sore thumb in a sea of Hondas, Toyotas and Kias. McKinley just shook it out of her head as she ran after Koran.

She could hear Koran's footsteps as they ran up the stairs to her fifth floor apartment.

"Koran!" She yelled after him as she ran. He was at least two floors ahead of her and he didn't sound like he was stopping. McKinley could hear the door leading from the stairwell to her floor swing open, and Koran's heavy footsteps as he ran to her apartment.

McKinley picked up the pace and when she finally reached her floor she expected to hear some screaming, fighting or crying, but it was eerily quiet. A chill went down her spine, and the hairs on the back of her neck stood up. She approached her door and saw that it was cracked open.

She entered her apartment and was immediately horrified. She fell against her door, shutting it behind her. A man stood there with one hand over Harlow's mouth and a gun pressed to the top of her head. "Oh my God!" McKinley yelled. She looked around and saw that Koran had frozen in horror as he watched his daughter shake from fear. Tears ran from her eyes and over the man's hand that gripped her mouth tightly. A few feet behind him was Ashley, staring intently at McKinley. McKinley looked around her apartment and saw Kristen sitting on the couch, looking nervous with her hands up in a surrendering stance.

As much as McKinley wanted to stop looking at the man, horrified, her eyes kept on going to him. He had such a despicable smile on his face, like he was receiving such pleasure from tormenting Harlow. The man couldn't break his glance from Koran.

"So you think you let me live, huh, nigga?"

"O, God so help you, if you don't let go of my child," Koran threatened. McKinley had never heard his tone in that way, it was low, menacing, and full of malice. "Let her go and take me, that's what all of this is for, right? Kill me!"

O cocked the hammer back, and everyone in the room jumped due to fear. "Oh, I'll let her go, motherfucker. You want her? Come get her!"

McKinley covered her face.

The sound of gun fire exploded in the room, along with a loud thump. "Oh my God!" Koran yelled.

McKinley yelled in in her hands. She couldn't bear to look at what O did. *I can't believe that he killed her! He killed that little girl!* McKinley thought horrified. She could feel her knees feel like they were about to buckle.

"Daddy!" Harlow's voice rang through the apartment and McKinley quickly looked up. Harlow ran to Koran and hugged him. He picked her up, crying and cradling her.

"Oh my God! Thank You God! Oh my God!" He kept on chanting as he rocked her.

"What just happened?" McKinley wondered aloud. She looked and saw that O's body was face down on the floor. An entrance wound from a gun was in the back of his head as a tiny stream of smoke slowly cascaded from it.

McKinley shrieked in horror. Her hands flew to her face and she recoiled in horror. She was shocked to feel the tears on her face.

"Shut the fuck up."

McKinley looked in the direction that the voice was coming from. It was Ashley's. Ashley had a gun pointed directly at McKinley.

McKinley's fright and surprise returned. She felt like her veins were pumping battery acid as adrenaline shot through her body. She had never been more aware of her surroundings in her entire life. It had been as if time slowed down, and everything was enhanced. The sound of her neighbors running out of the apartment due to the gunfire seemed to echo in her ears. The smell of gun powder seemed to sting her nostrils. The feel of her tears dripping off of her chin felt like she was face deep in a river, and her mouth tasted bizarrely dry.

Koran pushed Harlow into the bathroom, shut the door, and barricaded it with his body. "Ashley, what are you doing?"

Ashley eyed McKinley more intensely, "I'm just repaying a favor." She kicked O's dead body while maintaining eye contact with McKinley, "This piece of shit killed my cousin, Beans. I'm very protective of my family, especially my fiancé."

Kristen's eyes became wide. "Oh. My. God. You're the girl from the phone! The one I called in Miami! You're T!"

"Tanay?" McKinley finally uttered. She was shocked by how shaken her voice sounded.

"Yes, I'm Tanay." Ashley let them know.

"Why are you here? Why are you doing this?" McKinley said, sobbing and keeping eye contact with Tanay. She was afraid that if she dropped eye contact with her then Tanay would shoot her.

"Why did you distract Jamil while we were making our deal?" Tanay spat at McKinley. McKinley's eyes widened with surprise. "I was his down bitch. I was his partner. And I was there when you kept on fuckin' calling him and texting when we had an important deal to make."

Everything began to connect for McKinley. She was on the phone with Jamil when he was shot. She didn't understand why he was whispering before, but she now knew why he couldn't talk to her. "Oh my God."

"Me and that nigga had plans!" Tanay yelled. "We were raising our family together, living the high life and everything, and it all went away after you kept on pressing him. He told you he couldn't talk, but you kept on demanding him to! Now, I'm left alone with my kid, while you went on with your life!"

A loud knock sounded on McKinley's door. "Apartment security, what's going on in there? There were reported gunshots, is everyone okay? Police are on their way."

McKinley shook her head, "You got to believe me, Tanay, Jamil was no good. He was playing all of us."

Tanay approached McKinley, "Don't tell me nothing about Jamil!" She pounded her chest with her free hand. "He was my life! You just used him for his money and his gifts!" Tanay pressed the gun against McKinley's head.

McKinley cried harder, "I promise I didn't. I loved him, too. I thought he loved me. He proposed! If I knew about you then I wouldn't have stayed with him." McKinley pleaded for her life.

The sound of someone's shoulder banging into the door repeatedly rang through the apartment.

This is it. This is how I'm gonna die? Oh my God, I'm not

ready for this yet. Please, Jesus! McKinley closed her eyes and prepared for whatever was to come, until she felt the gun quickly leave her head. A loud crash was heard. McKinley opened her eyes to see what happened and was shocked when she saw Koran wrestling with Tanay for the gun.

Koran finally snatched the gun from her hands, but before he could restrain Tanay she bit down hard on his hand. Koran let out a bellowing yell of pain. The door finally burst open, right when the sound of a gun shot rang through the apartment again.

"Koran!" McKinley yelled.

Security rushed in and began to restrain everyone. McKinley looked around to see what was going on as all of the voices melted together. "Koran! Koran?" McKinley yelled.

XoXo

Police walked around the apartment. McKinley sat on her couch, crying with Kristen rubbing her back and Harlow on the other side of her, hugging McKinley.

A policeman was walking through, and talking into his radio. "Two confirmed homicides," was all that McKinley heard as she continued to cry.

Another policeman approached the three on the couch. "So who delivered the fatal wounds?"

Kristen pointed to O's body, "Well, Ashley... I mean, the

girl, Tanay, she killed him, and I killed the girl."

"Do you all mind coming with us to make a statement?" the police officer asked.

"Yeah, we will," Kristen answered for all of them.

As they headed out of the apartment, Koran was standing in the hallway as an EMT was treating the bite on his hand. Harlow ran to him and hugged him. He hugged her and picked her up with his free hand.

"I love you, Daddy!" Harlow cried to him.

"I love you too, so much, baby. So much!" Koran said, with his eyes closed, savoring every second he had with his daughter.

A policeman came behind McKinley and Kristen and blocked her view of Koran. "Misses, please? We need to get you to the station to make a statement."

McKinley nodded, and turned around and walked toward the elevator. As they got on, her and Koran's eyes met just as the doors were closing.

Epilogue

McKinley sat in a leather chair. Her fingers nervously picked at the seam on the arm of the chair. Across from her was her therapist, Veronica Collins. McKinley had been seeing her for the past two years, to help her deal with the trauma of everything that happened. Malik told her about Veronica while he tried to get over his feelings of trust and betrayal from Vanessa. Though Vanessa told him how O manipulated her, Malik couldn't trust her, and had difficulties trusting anyone except Koran and McKinley.

"So how are you feeling today, McKinley?" Veronica asked.

McKinley looked up at Veronica, she had such a warm smile, and it made McKinley smile. "I mean, I'm okay. I still get scared, especially at night." McKinley moved her hands to her maxi dress. It was decorated with brightly colored flowers. Her hair was bone straight and McKinley kept on pushing it off of her cheeks.

"That's understandable, you went through a lot."

McKinley looked around the room and noticed the sketch of "In the Box," the same sketch she bought from the art museum when she and Koran went on that perfect date. Her eyes began to water. It always happened whenever she saw that sketch.

"I think that I'm just frustrated because I thought that I would be over this by now. Why is it coming back so strongly now?" McKinley began to nervously rub the arms on the chair again.

"Usually," Veronica started while crossing her legs, "something like a transition can bring up past trauma. You're about to make a couple of big changes in your life, so it's natural that those past fears will reemerge."

"I hate feeling like this," McKinley admitted flatly.

Veronica leaned forward. "I understand, but it'll take some time. You've made great progress from the first time we started meeting. Remember what we discussed about the picture?" Veronica pointed to "In the Box."

McKinley exhaled and looked at the sketch. "Yeah, you were saying that how life is all about decisions. How the woman could either choose to be free or trapped, and how I have that same decision."

Veronica nodded. "Exactly, life is all about perception. You can either be trapped with your fears, or emerge from them."

"But, what if I fail?" McKinley said, rubbing her stomach, feeling nauseous.

Veronica looked alarmed and grabbed a package of saltines from her desk and handed it to McKinley. Once McKinley ate a few and seemed like she was calming down, Veronica sat back in her seat. "But, what if you succeed?"

McKinley looked up at Veronica while chewing loudly on a cracker.

"I feel that if nothing else, this whole situation has taught you that while you can't control other people, you have more control over your wellbeing than you realized." Veronica smiled at McKinley.

McKinley smiled back. She felt slightly more hopeful. McKinley looked at the clock. "Well, I guess I'll see you next week?"

"Of course," Veronica assured her. She went over to McKinley and helped her out of the chair. As McKinley got up, her pregnant stomach protruded under her dress. "Wait, your ring is caught," Veronica mentioned as she untangled McKinley's wedding ring from her sweater.

"Sorry," McKinley told her sheepishly.

"No problem. See you next week."

McKinley opened up the door to the waiting room and saw Koran and Harlow sitting there waiting for her. He smiled at her.

"How you doing?" he asked as she approached him. He pulled her in and gave her a quick kiss.

"I'm good. Just hungry and tired."

Harlow rubbed McKinley's stomach. "What does my little

brother want?" She placed her ear up to McKinley's stomach as if the fetus was talking to her. "What? You say you want some pizza?"

McKinley laughed. "Yes, that's exactly what he wants," she hugged Harlow.

The three left the therapist's building and walked to the car. As they approached, McKinley couldn't help but reflect on the major changes that her life had made. A few years ago she was selfish, only caring for herself, and in an emotionally stunted relationship. But after meeting Koran, finishing college, marrying Koran, getting pregnant and starting her own boutique, she saw just how strong she could be. She and Harlow became incredibly close, and she couldn't believe how easily she transitioned into the role of stepmom.

As Koran helped her into the passenger seat and closed the door, she began to feel as though she might never forget what happened to her, but she wasn't going to let it conquer her. She realized that she was stronger than ever, and now with this new baby she was excited about the possibilities of putting someone else first while still taking care of herself. Before, she always felt like she had to live for a man, but now her life was for her family, and she couldn't be happier.

Need more Keisha?
Check out Inhibitions
(see chapter 1 of "You
belong to Me" below)

You Belong To
Me

By

Keisha Ervin

Dedication

This story is dedicated to all of the hopeless romantics. Who know the love of your life might be right underneath your nose.

Prologue: 2008

After a long, brutal day of receiving verbal bitch slaps from her boss, line assistant, Nicolette Williams, sat irritably awaiting her blind date Kenzo. They were scheduled to meet at 7:00 PM at Miso, a sushi restaurant in St. Louis, for dinner, but it was 7:20 and Kenzo hadn't arrived or called to say he would be running late. If it hadn't been for her best friend, Madison's, big approval rating of him, Nik would have been stepped. Besides that, it had been months since Nik had been on a date so she was in desperate need for some male companionship.

There was only so much her rabbit vibrator could do. Although it satisfied the itch that needed to be scratched, a vibrator couldn't whisper naughty words in her ear, kiss her lips, or kneed her breasts. A woman needed physical contact and if Kenzo played his cards right, he might be the man to get inside of Nik's warm honey pot. Beyond annoyed by his tardiness, Nik gazed down at her watch, 7:30 PM.

This fool got five more minutes and I'm out. Then, as she took a small sip of her water, the door to the restaurant swung open and a tall drink of chocolate milk came walking through the door. Nik couldn't believe her eyes. Madison said he was fine but goddamn, this man was fine beyond words. He was six feet tall and looked to be almost two hundred pounds. Spinning waves ran throughout his jet black hair. Smoldering almond-shaped eyes, a regal nose, and a goatee made up his facial features.

Physically, he was one of God's greatest creations. But his attire, to Nik, was less than desirable. Kenzo looked like a twenty-eight-year-old stickup kid. Since it was winter, he rocked a blue Yankee's cap, a blue oversized hoodie with a tee shirt on underneath, baggy denim jeans, and a pair of wheat Timberland boots. Nik didn't know whether to duck for cover or introduce herself. Deciding to go with the latter, she stood up and smoothed down her skirt. Despite his appearance, Nik found herself unable to take her eyes off the huge bulge in the center of his jeans. That let her know he was working with a monster. *Maybe I won't have to cuss Madison out after all.*

"What up, chocolate?" Kenzo took her into his arms and hugged her tight.

Nik wasn't the type of chick that he normally went for because of her minimal makeup and conservative attire, but beyond the blah exterior, he couldn't get pass how stunningly beautiful she was. Nik was a 5'9" statuesque Barbie doll with skin the color of Godiva chocolate. Her long, coal black hair was pulled back into a single ponytail that reached the middle of her back. She possessed doe-shaped eyes and sensuous lips that he yearned to kiss.

"It's Nik. My name is Nik." She stepped back. "And you must be Kenzo." She gave him a half-hearted smile.

"Yep, that's my government, but you can call me Zo." He took a seat.

"Kenzo's fine," Nik replied, taken aback that he didn't pull out her chair. "You do realize that you're a half an hour late." She sat down and placed her napkin across her lap.

"My bad. I got caught up in the studio."

"Oh, so you're one of those?" Nik rolled her eyes.

"One of what?" Kenzo said perplexed.

"A rapper?"

"No, I'm an actor. I had to do some voice-over work. I just got a small role in this movie called *Precious*. I used to get into rap but the acting bug bit me," Kenzo said.

"Oh… isn't that special." Nik looked over the menu unimpressed.

Noticing the sour expression on her face, Kenzo said, "What? You got something against rappers?"

"No, as a matter of fact, I'm a huge fan of rap. Every now and then I'll bust out a lil' Will Smith or LL."

"You do realize its 2008, don't you?" Kenzo looked at her in disbelief. "You don't listen to Wayne or Kanye?"

"Absolutely not." Nik shook her head. "Lil' Wayne is a cough syrup sippin,' Bob Marley wannabe; and Kanye is a narcissistic, arrogant, asshole."

"Wow." Kenzo chuckled, outdone. "On that note, have you ordered yet?"

"No. I was trying to be polite and wait on you," Nik shot back sarcastically.

"That's what's up," Kenzo said oblivious to her dig. "Ay yo, Garcon." He snapped his fingers, signaling the waiter.

"You have got to be kidding me." Nik covered the side of her face with her hand, embarrassed.

"Sir?" the waiter said.

"Let me get a Hennessey and coke," Kenzo instructed. "What you want, Miss Lady?"

"Nik, my name is Nik," she said. "I'll have a Sprite, please." She looked at the waiter.

"Coming right up." The waiter nodded.

"You don't drink?" Kenzo was surprised.

"No."

"I bet that's not your real hair either." He smirked.

"Actually it is." Nik screwed up her face.

"Word? What you take like pregnancy pills or something to get it that long?" Kenzo leaned forward and eyed her quizzically.

"No." Nik's upper lip curled.

"Oh." Kenzo shrugged his shoulders and sat back in his chair.

"This is gonna be a long night," Nik mumbled.

"What you say?"

"Nothing." Nik waved him off.

"So why you think yo' homegirl wanted to set us up?" Zo sat back in his seat.

"I have no idea. I've been wondering why this entire time."

"Real talk, me too. I mean, yo' homegirl hella cool. She's a good look for Keith."

"Keith is a great guy. How are you two friends? Because you two are just … so different," Nik said, dying to know.

"He's my brother. And how are we so different?"

"Keith's just so refined—"

"Keep-A-Bitch Keith?" Kenzo chuckled. "Please, Keith is just as hood as I am."

"I find that hard to believe," Nik scoffed.

"Then you don't know Keith then. And what you trying' to say? 'Cause he work on Wall Street and wear a suit and a tie every day that he better than me?" Kenzo was offended.

"You said it. I didn't." Nik arched her eyebrow.

"See, this why I don't do shit like this. 'Cause bourgeoisie chicks like you get under my skin," he barked.

"I'm far from bourgeoisie, sweetheart." Nik folded her arms across her chest.

"Man, please. The stick you got up yo' ass is so long its choking' you!"

Nik's jaw instantly dropped. "You know what?" She

slapped down her napkin on the table. People around them stared but she didn't care. She'd had enough. It was time to put Kenzo in his place once and for all. "I have better things to do with my time then to sit here and be attacked! First, you were late. You have no manners and you're dressed like a reject from *The Wire*. So frankly, my dear, you can kiss my ass!" Nik scooted back her chair.

"What ass? I've seen fatter asses on Asian women." Kenzo laughed.

Appalled, Nik gasped for air. "Fuck you!" she hissed, grabbing her purse.

"I'm good shorty. You're not my type." Kenzo waved her off.

"That's the first thing you've said all night that we can agree on." Nik stood up. "Goodnight douche bag!"

"That's why you look like Condoleezza Rice, trick," Kenzo yelled over his shoulder as she stormed out.

ONE

Three Years Later

"Uh-uh-uh," Nik moaned while riding up and down on her boyfriend Greg's dick.

For almost thirty minutes she'd tried her damnest to cum but the closer she came to bliss the quicker it seemed to disappear. Maybe it was because she was about to come face to face with her arch nemesis after three years. Since their date from hell, she'd moved to New York and became an executive producer for the Ego network and created such hits for the network like *The Millionaire Wives' Club, Skeezer Scavenger Hunt*, and *Who Wants to Be a Porn Star*?

Nik wished she could've produced more profound pieces, but reality shows made money and the network wanted hits. So despite her vast knowledge of politics, foreign policies, and documentary work, she had to deliver. Greg, on the other hand, despised her work and begged her on numerous occasions to quit and allow him to take care of her. But Nik was no kept woman. Since birth she'd been raised to be self-sufficient.

Sure Greg had more money than Brad Pitt and Beyoncé combined, but none of that mattered to Nik. She loved him for his charming ways, debonair style, and take-control attitude. Unlike Nik, he'd grown up wealthy. Greg was like the black John F. Kennedy Jr. His father was a judge for the Supreme Court and his mother was hotelier and socialite Judith Steiner.

Greg, himself, was the other owner and CEO of his very own energy drink. He was everything a woman could dream for. He was rich, powerful, and handsome, but no matter how much Nik tried to ignore it, there was just something messing between them.

"Lay down." Greg grabbed her waist and laid her on her back.

In the missionary position, Nik wrapped her arms around Greg's neck. With her eyes closed, she tried to match his rhythm in order to cum, but once again she became distracted.

"What time is it?" she said.

Greg looked over at the clock. "Six o'clock, why?" He panted.

"We need to hurry up. I have a million things to do."

"You're joking, right?" Greg looked at her face.

"No, so nut now or forever hold your peace." Nik patted his back.

"Can you please find another word to use besides nut? It's so crass." Greg continued to stroke.

"Sorry, can you please ejaculate so we can go?" Nik rolled her eyes.

While Greg rolled his hips in a circular motion and worked her middle, all Nik could think about was finishing packing, making sure she had her passport, getting to the airport on time, and arriving at Neckar Island for her best friend Madison and Keith's wedding. It was too bad she'd have to share the wonderful occasion with Kenzo.

"Ooh," Greg groaned, pumping faster, causing Nik's head to hit the headboard.

"I'm cumming," he said.

Not in the least bit turned on, Nik gazed at the wall in anticipation of him finishing and her getting up.

"Ah," Greg groaned as his body shuttered and he came. "Whew." He pulled out of her and slumped over onto his side. "I don't know about you, but I feel great." He smiled.

"Good for you." Nik stood up and put on her robe. "Now get up. We don't have any more time to waste. We have to pack our suitcases, shower, dress, and make it to the airport in less than an hour and a half." Nik went into her closet and pulled out her Louis Vuitton luggage.

"I didn't know us making love was wasting time, but all right." Greg got up, slightly pissed.

"I wasn't saying it like that, honey." Nik tried to clean it up.

"It's okay." Greg went into the bathroom to throw away the condom they'd used.

"No, it's not." Nik took his hand once he returned to the room. "I apologize. I'm just so overwhelmed."

"I know you are. That's why you have to calm down. This is supposed to be a relaxing five day vacay."

"For you but not for me. I still have the bachelor/bachelorette party to plan since Kenzo hasn't lifted a finger to help, except for writing a check. As a matter of fact, let me call him now and see if he's hired the belly dancers like he promised."

"Don't you think it's a bit early?" Greg said.

"I don't care. He should be up anyway." Nik dialed his number. "I'll probably speak to his assistant anyway since he won't bother to speak to me himself."

"Hello? This is Kenzo Porter's assistant Janet, how may I help you?"

"Good morning, Janet, this is Nik. Is Kenzo available?"

"Actually." Janet paused. "He's not. Is there anything that I can help you with?"

"Yes. I wanted to know if he's hired the belly dancers for the bachelor/bachelorette party yet? The party is just days away."

"Um, I don't think so, but I will make sure that it is taken care of."

"Please do, Janet. I would really appreciate it."

"No problem, and let me know if there is anything else I can help you with."

"I probably will, knowing your boss," Nik said, hanging up. "Ugh! I can't stand him!" She raised her hands to the sky.

"What?" Greg said, while picking out underwear.

"He hasn't done anything I've asked him to do. I swear to God when I see him I might punch him in the face." Nik fought the air.

"You will do no such thing." Greg held her by her arms. "Kenzo is a very busy man. He's the highest paid actor in the world right now. I'm sure he doesn't have time to plan some stupid party."

"Um, excuse me, but my best friend's bachelorette party is not stupid." Nik removed his hands from her arms. "And Kenzo isn't any busier than I am. I know it's not a big deal to you, but I do run one of televisions' biggest networks."

"Your words not mine." Greg went into the bathroom and turned on the shower.

"Whatever. Just hurry up so we can go!"

* * *

"Kenzo! Kenzo!" Janet nudged his back. "Kenzo wake up! You're going to miss your flight!"

"Huh?" He scrunched up his face and tried opening his eyes.

"You have to get up. The car is outside waiting for you."

"I'm up. I'm up." Kenzo turned onto his side and spotted a

naked Hispanic woman asleep.

"Whoa," he said, sitting up only to find a caramel cutie at the foot of his bed.

"Baby, where are you going?" The white woman on his left whined.

Kenzo had no recollection of bedding the three beauties the night before. The whole night was an entire blur. But from the looks of his bedroom, he had a hell of a time. There were red plastic cups, beer bottles, lube, a set of handcuffs, and Magnum Trojan condoms scattered everywhere.

"Yeah, the rest of the house looks even worse," Janet said, reading his mind.

"Cool." Kenzo grinned, pleased with himself.

"Come on, you're running super late." Janet urged out of bed.

"Okay." Kenzo got out of bed.

"No, baby, come back." The Hispanic woman pouted. "Don't you wanna play with these?" She pressed her titties together.

"I wish I could but I gotta go right now." Kenzo eyed her big luscious breasts.

"Aw, no fair." The Hispanic woman hit the pillow with a fist.

"Enough of this foolishness, you have to get in the shower now or you won't make it to your brother's wedding." Janet pushed Kenzo toward the master bath.

"Oh, and by the way, Nik called again. You forgot to tell me to hire belly dancers for the party."

"Damn, I did," Kenzo said, taking off his boxer briefs.

"Do you have any shame?" Janet covered her eyes and turned around.

"Not when I look this good." Kenzo admired his muscular frame in the mirror.

"I've seen better," Janet teased.

"Who you foolin'?" Kenzo smirked.

Janet simply smiled because she knew he was right. "Anyway, she seemed pretty upset."

"That sounds about right." Kenzo turned on the hot water.

"You have exactly ten minutes to shower and dress," Janet said, closing the door behind her.

Kenzo opened the shower door and got in. The hot, steamy water instantly woke him up and made him wish Nik was enjoying the sensation with him. It had been three years since they'd come face to face. But images of her angelic face often resurfaced in his mind. Sure, on the night of their date he'd been a dick and she'd been an uppity bitch. But beyond her holier-than-thou attitude, he saw a woman full of potential.

Physically she was a ten. It was her mouth he couldn't get with. He wondered if after all this time she'd changed and loosened up a bit. But by the sound of Janet's messages she hadn't.

Kenzo just prayed they'd be able to get along long enough to support her best friend and his brother during the biggest moment of their lives without killing each other.

* * *

"Wow, this is beautiful," Nik gleamed, stepping down off of the boat.

Neckar Island, Billionaire Richard Branson's villa, where Madison and Keith's nuptials would take place, was breathtaking. It was completely secluded and every couples' dream wedding location. It was a seventy-four acre, private, paradise on the British Virgin Islands. The main house where all of the guests were staying held ten bedrooms, an indoor and outdoor dining area, Balinese-styled interiors for lounging, and a reading and games area with a full-size snooker table.

A staff of thirty-one was there to pamper the guests at all times. Nik couldn't wait to let her hair down and enjoy all of the amenities the villa had to offer. Holding Greg's hand, she led him across the pristine white sand to greet Madison and Keith.

"Friend!" Madison extended her arms wide and ran toward Nik.

"Bestie!" Nik held out her arms as well.

"I missed you." Madison hugged her tight.

"I missed you too." Nik held her at arm's length and gazed

at her lovingly.

"Do you love it or do you love it?" Madison gushed.

"This is sick, Maddie. I mean, beyond fab*u*lous." Nik was in awe. "And look at you. You look great."

Maddie was a pint-sized caramel cutie. Her entire being exuded sex appeal and her attire often reflected it. The purple halter beach dress she rocked highlighted her 34 D breast implants and showcased enough leg to make any red blooded man look twice.

"I try." Madison posed like a supermodel. "You, on the other hand, friend, look a hotmess.com. What happened to your hair?"

"I don't know." Nik tried to control her mane unsuccessfully. "It just poofed up like an afro. This heat is ridiculous, girl. I'm sweating like Whitney Houston on stage." She fanned her armpits.

"Um-mm." Greg cleared his throat.

"Oh, babe, I'm sorry." Nik took him by the hand and pulled him toward her. "Madison, this is my boyfriend, Greg that I've gone on and on about; and, Greg, this is my best friend, Madison."

"Nice to meet you. I've heard so much about you." He greeted her with a warm hug.

"So have I, and I would like for you to meet my soon-to-be-husband Keith." Madison smiled up at her fiancé.

"Nice to meet you." Keith shook his hand.

"We have so much to go over." Madison's sweet demeanor vanished and a more serious side of her appeared. "There is so much more that needs to be done and my wedding planner, honey, is working' my nerves."

"I got you. Everything's gonna be fine. You're gonna have the most beautiful wedding ever, I promise," Nik swore.

"Thanks, girl. I needed that."

"Uh-oh, here comes trouble." Keith boasted, looking toward the ocean.

Nik followed his gaze and found Kenzo along with a few other guests getting off of another boat.

This shit isn't fair, Nik thought. While she looked like a refugee, Kenzo looked as if he'd stepped right out of an ad campaign. The man looked better than he did three years before. Money and fame really agreed with him. Instead of rocking' waves in his hair, he now sported a low cut and his goatee had been replaced with a full, luscious beard that framed his kissable lips well.

Damn, I wanna kiss him. Nik gazed at him absentmindedly. *No you don't! Remember, he's an asshole? Okay, get it together. He is not all that.* Smoothing her hair back for the one hundredth time, Nik plastered on a fake smile as Kenzo neared.

"What up, nigga?" Kenzo greeted Keith with a hug.

"You, Mr. Box Office." Keith hugged him back. "Me and Madison just went to see *Unbreakable*. You did yo' thang, man."

"Yeah, they say I might get nominated for a Golden Globe."

"Oh, most definitely."

"Excuse me, Mr. Porter, but can I please have your autograph?" one of Madison's bridesmaids nervously said.

Nik wanted to hate on the chick but she was gorgeous. The woman was everything Nik wasn't. She was short and built like a brick house.

"Damn." Greg admired her frame. He was eyeing her so hard he was practically drooling.

"Excuse you." Nik nudged him.

"What?" He shrugged, trying to play it off.

"Who do you want me to make this out to, sweetheart?" Kenzo stared deep into the woman's eyes.

"Laila." The woman swooned.

"You got a piece of paper, Miss Laila?"

"No. You can sign right here." Laila pulled the neck of her top to the side, revealing the upper part of her right breast.

"I think I'm gonna throw up." Nik rolled her eyes unaware that Kenzo heard her.

"Ay, Keith? You smell that?" Kenzo sniffed the air, handing Laila back her pen.

"Smell what?" Keith looked around curiously.

"I smell a hater in the air." Kenzo shot daggers at Nik with his eyes. "What's up, junk in the trunk?"

"For the millionth time, my name is Nik," she snapped.

"Oh my bad, Nicole."

"It's Nicolette, fool!"

"Whatever, it's all the same," Kenzo teased.

"Are you two gonna fight the whole time?" Madison said, hugging Kenzo.

"That's her." He pointed like a child.

"What are you, nine?" Nik curled her upper lip.

"No, but my dick is." Kenzo cracked up laughing.

"All right, that's it." Nik threw up her hands defeated. "I'm going to my room! Greg!" she yelled over her shoulder as she stormed off.

"But I haven't even got to speak to Kenzo yet. You know I'm a huge fan."

"Are you insane?" Nik whispered, walking into his personal space. "The man just insulted me."

"Well, you did kinda start it." Greg shrugged.

"You know what? Do you!" Nik spat, grabbing her own luggage.

"It was nice meeting you all." Greg picked up his bags and ran after Nik.

"You better leave my friend alone." Madison laughed.

"She'll be a'ight." Kenzo waved his hand dismissively.